To Live & Die in LA 2
By Terry L. Wroten

I0655595

Copyright © 2016 by No Brakes Publishing

Published in the United States by No Brakes Publishing

PUBLISHER'S NOTE

Chapter 1

"Yard down! "Yard down!" The tower cop yelled, "Yard down!" repeatedly, as an inmate called Butch, fatally stabbed a jailhouse rat. Dee Bastard shook his head at the terrifying sight. He thought back to his first bid and how he had killed Brother Bilal for running his mouth. Looking at Butch penetrate the rat, in and out with his homemade shank brought tears to Dee Bastard's eyes. Butch was a soldier. A loyal soldier for what he believed in and fought for. But what the young soldier didn't realize was he had just thrown his life away for some dudes who, at the end of the day, would never be loyal to him.

The turtles swarmed the yard and pounced on Butch like football players all going for the ball. Canisters of pepper spray and batons were heavy at work. Dee Bastard turned his head, wanting to desperately go help Butch, but he wanted no part of the losing stick. Nonetheless, he could not stand the thought that he had somehow found himself back incarcerated after his seven-year bid, which he only stayed free for a few days.

As Dee Bastard laid prone on the ground, he couldn't help but think how he couldn't last on the streets. After all those lectures from the old man, Brother Ajene, along with all those promises he made to his mother, the "I'm going to do better" letters. Even after the soul searching, Dee Bastard could not stay out of the human warehouse.

Tears flooded his eyes in rivers. "What happened to me getting out and making momma proud?" he thought. "What happen to me getting out and becoming a bestselling author? What happened to me starting my own publishing company? What happened to me getting out and living righteous, and starting a life with Laurell? Dee Bastard was in deep thought as the turtles rushed Butch off the yard in handcuffs. The rat's body laid lifeless a few feet away from him.

Dee Bastard laid in defeat. His spirit was crushed. He was an outcast! He was one of societies throw aways, one who would never amount to anything. Before leaving prison, he thought he had learned his lesson. He was terrified at the thought of breaking the law or even coming back to jail. "Damn, how the fuck I lost focus so easy?" he asked himself.

Dee Bastard was going through it. The initial shock of being back incarcerated was death within itself. He planted his face in his palm and cried. You would have thought he had lost a loved one in the jailhouse rat, but it was the thought of not amounting to anything. The thought of when those penitentiary doors opened after seven long years. The thought of not being able to soar like a free

4

bird, but to be recaptured like a runaway slave. Those bottled up emotions would drive Dee Bastard into a depression where he would contemplate suicide day in and day out.

Chapter 2

"Don't nobody fuckin' move! This is a robbery!"

As Dee Bastard laid, captured in a prison cell, P and Sheik, two of his young protégées, were tearing up the streets of Los Angeles. With Dee Bastard gone once again, these two goons and known stick up kids, had to take matters into their own hands.

P met Dee Bastard when he was twelve and Dee Bastard was seventeen. They met in Central Juvenile Halls when Dee Bastard was in his third year of his seven-year sentence for robbery. P was a car thief at the time, whom Dee Bastard took under his wings instantly. The two juveniles hit it off right away and were close ever since. Things had changed, P resented Dee Bastard. He felt Dee Bastard was confused. After seven years in prison, he was not the same. Dee Bastard went from being the leader and founder of the infamous TLB clique, who was known for robbing, selling drugs, killing, and gangbanging.

At the early age of fourteen, Dee Bastard along with his best friend Pedro Guzman, aka Bastard Child, BC for short, got their first stolen car, first pistol, and first heist on a well-known jeweler. The pair had fat, gold chains and a lot of money. They used the stolen cars and pistols they acquired from the various heists. Before forming the TLB clique, Dee Bastard, and BC were recruited into a sub-chapter of the Crips organization, the 4 Trey Gangsta Crips.

For most kids growing up in the city of Los Angeles making it to the NBA or NFL was like hitting the lottery. Ghetto superstars, black supermen, drug dealers, gangbangers, and stick up kids were the heroes around here.

Dee Bastard and the clique were P's idols. All three, above and put on for the city. From Dee Bastard to BC to fallen soldiers such as Dynasty. The TLB's shaped most young kids growing up on the block views. But Dee Bastard was a standup guy. Cats knew him all across Los Angeles from putting in work on the streets and in the penitentiary. However, to P, Dee Bastard had changed. He was different. One minute he preached against the street life and hitting niggas on the head. Then the next minute, he was contemplating his next murder. It was a struggle that Dee bastard had to go through that none of his goons could understand.

"Bitch, I said this is a robbery!" P yelled, grabbing the manager by the collar.

P ushered her to where the money was located, inside the vault at the EZ Cash Check Cashing.

Sheik cleared all of the drawers for whatever contents he could get. Boo Boo, another stick-up kid from around the projects they grew up in, had the floor crowd under control. The trio had already unarmed the security guards and backed all the cashiers from the counters.

Like clockwork, P strolled out of the vault with a duffle bag filled with money and his tech nine dangling at his side. The trio slipped out of the establishment with ease. They had done this before. It had become natural to them.

Later that night, after P and his crew had made it and each grossed 32,000 from their heist. He and his on and off girlfriend, Kioshi, laid in bed talking. P pulled out a blunt of potent Kush.

"Percy, you know I love you, right?"

"Pssst." P almost choked. He knew Kioshi had more game than the Parker Brothers.

She was the love of his life, but it was no secret that she was a prostitute. Her motto was, you lay, you pay. Kioshi had been on the streets her whole life, so she had to get it how she lived. Her mother conceived her while turning a trick for a quick hit of crack cocaine, so she was cursed since birth. However, what most people did know was that she loved P, and Percy Jr loved her.

"Come on, Kiki, go on with the cap," P said. "The only reason you love me is because I just told you that I hit a lick. I mean, damn, if you love a nigga so much, where have you been these last few days. A nigga hasn't seen you since Dee Bastard's welcome home party."

"Boy, boo! First of all, I got more money than you, so I am not worrying about your little ass chump change. But I am happy for you. Second of all, I been laying low since the shootout. I don't want my name to be getting caught up in nothing like that."

P nodded while passing the blunt back to her. "Yeah, I agree. But least you don't got to worry about that fuck boy disrespecting you. I mean, disrespecting what's mine."

A snide grin stretched across Kioshi's face as she pulled on the blunt and let out a stream of smoke. "Yea it's yours alright. After all these years you still don't know what to do with me. You sho' ain't put a ring on these fingers."

"Ha! P laughed. "The last nigga who tried to put a ring on your finger is dead because he got rejected."

"No. Don't say it like that! Don't try to put that man murder on me. He got killed because he tried to be somebody that he was not."

9

"Okay. I hear you. But ask me do I believe you."

"Do you?"

"No!"

P put the blunt to his mouth after snatching it from Kioshi. Their bond was one out of this world. This young couple had been through a lot together. They were each other's match sent from heaven, but neither one of them were ready for a true commitment.

"Kioshi, fa real doe! You know I love you too. You gone always be my girl even if we are not together."

"Percy be quiet because you know just like I know we gone always be together."

"But oh yeah I forgot to ask you, have you talked to your friend Dee Bastard."

P furred his brows. "No. Why?" He had not heard from Dee Bastard since the night of the welcome home party when they had to kill Bo and Smooth. Then Dee Bastard went back to being strange talking about he's retiring from the street life, moving to New York, and starting a writing career and publishing company.

"Well," Kioshi said, "Trapstar told me that Big Wrap told him that the police raided Dee Bastard girlfriends' house and took him and that Mexican Crip to jail. But nobody knows why."

The news took P by surprise. He wanted to hop up and make a few calls to see if what Kioshi was talking about was true. But deep down inside he knew Kioshi was good at having the latest 4-1-1 on everything going on around L.A. They say, women hold the keys to opportunity because men confide in them by pillow talk, telling their deepest secrets; therefore this makes women the gatekeepers of opportunity. Due to Kioshi's occupation, she was prone to all the latest gossip.

At this point in time, P was high and horny. All he wanted to do was stick his dick in Kioshi and fall asleep. And Kioshi wanted just that. She leaped to her feet. Her banging body had P biting down on his bottom lip. Before they knew it, they were both in their birthday suits going at it like cats and dogs.

Kioshi was a red bone, and P considered himself a red bone lover. She was a black woman who looked to be every nationality. She laid down and started massaging her clit. P looked at the pretty pink pussy as it became moist and wet. Kioshi slid three fingers deep inside her. She knew how to get a man; especially Percy Jr.

P pulled out his dick and with the quickness dove right on top of Kioshi, missionary style.

"Fuck me good, Daddy!" Kioshi said.

"I'm bout to do just that," P replied.

Chapter 3

"This got to be the house," Detective Gilmore told himself as he pulled in front of a house on the lower eastside of Los Angeles. The house was dark. The windows were empty as a dead man's eyes. No light shone in nor out of the old wooden California Craftsman. The house looked as if it was something straight out of a scary movie. It had a foreboding darkness that not even the street lights could penetrate.

"Damn, I can't see shit, but this got to be the house."

Detective Gilmore tapped the pedal to the undercover car and sped up the block. He pulled into a space in front of a hydrant. He did this because he had no back-up. The one thing he knew he couldn't do was to call for back-up because he was up to no good. Detective Gilmore was known for bending and breaking a few laws to crack a case. He had even been suspended and transferred from the homicide special unit of LAPD Metropolitan Robbery-Homicide Division to Newton Division homicide squad. Detective Gilmore ranks weren't stripped away due to the fact that he was still praised for his heroic act of helping bring down the Notorious Crip leader, Killa Black. He was even glorified by the media as the detective who brought back peace to the community that the nuisance Bloods and Crips had terrorized. After the book "Natural Born Killaz" hit the bookstores and his fifteen minutes of fame played out, Detective Gilmore sought out to live that experience again. Now, armed with a new lead from the prostitute on a media-driven multiple homicide case, Gilmore was back in action.

After turning off the engine, he leaped from the car and jogged up the sidewalk. He pulled out his .357 revolver as he hurried back toward the darkened house. He quietly crept onto the porch which was a full front porch with a full picture window. No light nor movement showed through the glass. However, he could hear the whore moan and groan.

"Oh yes, Daddy!"

"Fuck me!"

"Fuck me!"

"Fuck me good!"

Gilmore smiled inwardly hearing the prostitute moan and groan. She said the same thing to him when he was in that pussy. Gilmore leaned against the railing of the porch, raised his right leg and kicked the door right above the knob.

"LAPD Freeze!"

The trick was on top of the whore fucking her good. Gilmore caught them off guard with the loud noise from the door being kicked open and the bright light from the flashlight and gun pointed at them. The man instantly jumped up to his feet with his hands up.

"Aww man, what is this? A nigga ain't even do nothing."

Gilmore saw the terror in his new informants' eyes. "Shut up and get dressed. You going down for questioning."

The man's eyes widened. "Questioning for what?"

Gilmore smiled inwardly still in the standard police stance with pistol and flashlight. "You know that shooting at the club that's been on the news every day, and about who killed Smooth and Bo at that hotel."

The man screwed his face. He looked at the whore then back at the detective. Something wasn't right. No one knew he was at the club but a hand full of people. The whore was one! Thoughts of the whole club shootout started an adrenaline rush through his body. This gave him clarity. The whore had set him up!

Chapter 4

"Okay, Momma Mary I have to get going. I'm gonna come back and check on you tomorrow," Shady said as he stood up from the kitchen table after eating a great home-cooked meal made by Dee Bastards mom.

Shady was Mary's adopted son. In all honesty, Mary was the hood mom for the TLB clique. Even though her son and his crew were monsters in the eyes of society, they were her babies. They were young black men who made a few bad choices after being dealt the wrong hands. She understood that they were products of their environment, products of their education and products of the information they took in while at home, in the hood, at school, or in the church. She understood that they, even her own flesh and blood, her son, struggled with finding themselves. They were young men with no identity. Young black men with no history of race. Every race of people has its own land except the black people. From Chinese to Koreans to Russians to Europeans to English to Irish to Africans. She often sympathized with her son and his friends, because she knew a race without history has no future. The only thing Dee Bastard and his friends had was Hip-Hop. Every time she watched a rap video, there it was: shoot 'em up bang-bang. Or Snoop Doggy

Dogg, as Mary called rapper Snoop Dogg, talking about it "Ain't No Fun If The Homies Can't Have None" or "Murder Was The Case".

As Mary stood at the sink washing dishes and putting the leftovers from the dinner she'd prepared up, she couldn't help but miss her son. Shady filled the void, but she needed Darrell to be home. "Okay, Andre. I hope you are full. If not, I made you a to go plate."

Shady smiled as he grabbed the to go plate. "Aww thank you, Momma Mary. I'll never be able to repay you for all the nights I needed a good home cooked meal and couldn't get one because I don't got a girl and my favorite girl is gone home with the man up above."

Mary walked over to Shady and hugged him tight. She knew out of all of Darrell's friends Shady had the brightest future, but since his mother died he had not been the same. In which she could not blame him.

"Andre, I want you to understand that your mother loved you and only wanted the best for you, I know things will never be the same for you because I feel the same way about Darrell. I mean he's not dead…"

"But he'd been gone the last seven years from home only to get out and not come see me…"

Mary paused again. This time tears filled her eyes and ran down her cheeks in rivers. "That boy made me all those promises! He promised me he was going to do better. I got the letters. I even got the ones I wrote him. What hurt the most that I knew he was home, the day he came. I thought he was going to come straight here the day he came home. I waited all day and all night for three days straight. And on the day he got arrested, I felt it in my heart because I woke up in the hospital. I had a heart attack. If it wasn't for my neighbor hearing the big boom from me hitting the ground I would have died in this house…"

Shady shook his head. He hated the fact that most of his friends took their mothers for granted. In his wildest of dreams, he only wished his mother was still alive. Not only that, but he regretted some of the things he did while she was living and wished he could have just apologized before she died. Shady knew you get one mother and you must treasure her.

"Don't cry momma Mary," Shady held Mary tight. "First chance I get imma go have a man to man talk with Dee. I know them people don't have nothing on him, so he will be home soon."

"Andre, that's the problem and please talk to him for me because he has to learn how to resist temptation or if not, this is going to be his destiny. Prison is going to be his home, and being out here

18

with us going to be a vacation. I know his past was calling him when he got out but he has been loyal and true to the streets for too long. You have to tell him he has to turn his back on everything and stand for what he believes in."

Shady nodded his head and agreed.

"I will do just that. I promise."

Mary broke their embrace. She was fighting for her son even when he didn't know it. She prayed on the issue daily, but she felt she had to do more than walk by faith to get her son back. And as far as his inner circle was concerned, Shady was the man to get at. He was gangsta yet gentle. He was wild yet tamed. He was hard yet soft. He was smart yet dumb. All in all, he was well respected and lived up to his name. He knew how to do his dirt and stay low key. If you didn't know Shady, you would have thought he was a school boy instead of the presiding general of the notorious TLB clique. The tattoo over his heart read: TLB or NOTHING! And he meant every word.

"Okay. Andre, but I want you to hear me on this because your word is your bond and even though yall call me the hood mama, I'm still Darrell's mother. I see stuff y'all can't see because y'all too busy caught up in the web of deceit and destruction. But here's the truth…"

"You, Darrell, and Pedro are stand up guys. Y'all did y'all work. Y'all did y'all dirt. Darrell and Pedro got caught, did their time, and kept their mouths shut. They kept to the 'G' code, but his mom had to bury him due to the hands of some people who didn't stick to the code. What I'm getting at is, you live by the gun, you die by the gun. But in today's time and with the new generation of gangsters, Crips, and Bloods, if you live by the gun you going to die in the cell. These kids will tell on their dying great-grandmom to escape a prison sentence. A major universal law I always preach to Darrell is: You're either growing or you're decaying. So as you walk out of these doors just think about what Momma Mary is telling you."

Shady nodded his head in agreement and made his way to the door. Outside, on the porch, night had fallen and dark clouds and fog hovered over the block making it hard to see. The only thing visible were the streetlights and the glow from the ground they reflected off of. Just as Shady took a step off the porch, a Caprice slowly crept up the block. The car moved at the pace of a snail. Whoever it was, they were up to no good. His street knowledge and expertise kicked in. he leaned back into the darkness against the railing of the porch. He left his pistol under the driver seat in his car. Out of respect for Dee Bastard, he couldn't sum up the courage to walk in his childhood friend's mom's house with a gun. The darkness shielded him from being seen, and Shady squinted his eyes to get a good look at the occupants. *Damn!* he thought, *That look like that crooked-ass detective. And damn is that the homie pointing this way at the house?*

Shady wasn't for sure if the dude in the Caprice with the detective was who he thought it was. But if it was, snitching was becoming a trend something he was not with.

As the car made its way off the block, Shady made a mental note to call Big Wrap so they could sit down and analyze what Mary put him on. And after seeing this, he knew Momma Mary wasn't lying. Snitching was at an all-time high.

Chapter 5

"Damn, I can't believe this nigga is back in jail," Laurell told no one in particular as she sat in her twin sister, Laurie's apartment. She sat sipping on a bottle of Grey Goose with her twin and her female companion, Kasey.

"He got out moving too fast," Laurie declared. "And you and Kasey didn't make things any better by keeping him locked in that house fucking and sucking his first 72 hours out. Y'all know he had to go check in with his parole officer."

Laurell put her hand in the air, signaling for Laurie to stop the press. "Smack!" she smacked her lips. "Laurie, go on with all the bullshit and tryna preach, because you had BC Mexican-ass, hostage too. But to keep it 100, I do wish we would have done things better and even said fuck a welcome home party."

"Girl, don't start stressing already. He might be home tomorrow. They don't even got him charged with anything yet," Kasey said. "All we know is they kicked down our door while we were gone and took them to jail. So far, everything is pointing towards a violation. Laurie, have you heard from BC yet because Dee Bastard still hasn't called. That's the reason Laurell is really stressing. And every time we check online he's not popping up, and when we call, they say they can't give any information on him yet."

"No. I haven't heard from BC," Laurie declared. "But I know the first chance they get they're going to be running the phone bill sky high."

"Well, they need to hurry up because I been literally sick to my stomach since my husband has been gone…"

Laurell had been sick to the stomach no doubt. She figured it was just the thought of knowing Dee Bastard was back in jail, but at this time, little did she know she was pregnant.

"I mean I thought the day he got out would never come. It was like I did seven years myself. I mean, I was lonely just like he was. I had to keep everything together for him. Like his lawyers, his commissary, his visits, his mail, his pussy. It was hard, lonely, and sad all rolled up in one. I thought I'd never have to experience him being in jail again. And when that day came I was anxious, nervous, and scared. And that's how I feel right now."

Laurell had tears rolling down her cheeks in rivers. It was just yesterday she was crying tears of joy. Yet these tears on this night were tears of disappointment, tears of depression, and tears of anger. Laurell was more upset with herself than anyone else. Most cats released from prison didn't have anything. No girl, no family, no money, or any transportation; and most of them lasted at least a week. Dee Bastard couldn't do that. To Laurell's logic, it was all her fault. She felt she didn't stick to the famous saying 'Behind every strong man, there's a strong woman'.

One key element that Laurell overlooked as she sat in sorrow, sipping herself into a drunken state of mind, is that Dee Bastard was a young man who made his own choices. No one put a gun to his head. Yes, as his woman, she could have tried to assist him in making better choices. But once Dee Bastard mind was made up, there was nothing she could do about it. Nothing else mattered! Not even the long nights he cried himself to sleep in prison begging God to forgive him and let him be free like a bird. Nor the long talks he had with Brother Ajene while in solitary confinement. Nor the long letters and promises he made to his mother.

Laurell sipped the fiery liquor and cried. She cried and sipped all night into the wee hours. Laurie and Kasey had eventually dozed off. Before she knew it the sun was peeping through the blinds. She was still up in sorrow and deep thought. She couldn't help but think back to how they got together. That was her favorite memory.

Summer of 1997

The first day of school at John Adams Middle school was a fashion show in which Darrell and his best friend Pedro Guzman, aka Bastard Child, planned on winning best dressed. They hopped out of Smooth's all-black 1986 Cutlass Supreme on eighteen-inch chrome 100 spoke rims. Shining like new money.

Smooth was their big brother in the streets. He was a ghetto superstar who taught the fatherless kids the hustle and bustle of the fast life in South Central. Most kids whose parents had grown up in the controlled territory of the 4-Trey's or gangs who allied with them, such as the East Coast Crips and the Harlem 30s, admired him just as their parents had. Smooth was the man, so hopping out of his car on the first day of school put Darrell and Pedro on every girl's scouting list. They could smell the juices from pussy trying to get their attention as soon as they exited the car, and so could the old pussy hound Smooth.

"Y'all two niggas don't dip into none of that young pussy without protection." He handed them both some condoms from the glove box. Smooth turned up the music, blasting "Love Is Gonna Getcha" by KRS-One, turning heads of all the star-struck little girls. "I'm out this bitch. Fo' minutes, Lil homies." He threw up the set and peeled out.

"Three seconds," Dee Bastard and BC called after him. Just as the two rising stars entered the school and walked through the hallway toward their lockers, the twins and their two running mates, Kiva and Lashonda, came prancing their way. Pedro smiled, "Cuz, we gonna fuck the twins one day. They know they wanna fuck us too."

Darrell chuckled. "I bet they do, but I don't know if they wanna fuck yo' ole Mexican-ass. Me, on the other hand, I'm the overweight lover. I'll dip my dick in young pussy and old pussy." He looked at one of the teachers slyly as she passed. "Cuz, you might as well call me Overweight Lover Heavy Dee."

Pedro's brown skin reddened. "Nigga, shut that shit up. Cuz, half the women you fucked are crackheads or Smooth's leftovers. At least I ain't gotta move my stomach to see my dick, ya fat Manny Fresh looking muthafucka!"

Dee sucked his teeth. "Whatever nigga, Manny Fresh get hella pussy too wit' all that bread them Cash Money niggas is sitting on."

"Hey, Fresh-Fresh-Fresh-Fresh," Laurie teased Dee, having overheard their conversation. She had a more outgoing personality, which was the only way you could tell the difference between her and her sister. She gave his outfit the once-over and smiled in approval. Darrell was dipped in FUBU gear from his fitted cap to his shoes, and sporting a two-and-one-half-inch wide Rolex herringbone around his neck.

"What it do, Laurie?" Darrell opened his locker. "I ain't the only one fresh because you and my future wife looking good as ever!"

Both the twins were wearing super-tight jeans that showed off their figures while their home girls Kiva and Lashonda sported booty shorts that left little to the imagination. Their crew was the most fly and sexiest in the school, but to Darrell, Laurell won the prize for boss bitch. Even though she and her sister were identical twins and sporting the same thing, Laurell had that extra little something that her sister Laurie lacked. She was the one Darrell wanted and constantly thought of. It was crazy to him, because even though he was a chubby young dude with a mini afro, he received major love from all the girls around school...except for Laurell. This is what troubled him the most because Laurell was the one he craved, but she constantly played the hard-to-get role. It was the fact that she didn't sweat him like the rest of the girls that made him want her more.

Laurie blushed at Darrell's future wife comment but rolled her eyes at the same time. She knew her sister was fronting. Laurell had a crush on Darrell, like every other girl in school, did. She sucked her teeth. "Mrs. Rell, don't act like that now. All the stuff you be talking at home about Darrell, you better say something." She put her sister on the spot.

Darrell picked up on her embarrassment and used it to his advantage. He swooped in and grabbed his dream girl about the waist. "Baby Girl, don't act like that with a tiny loc." He flashed his winning smile. "Shawty, gangstas got feelings too. We need a Lil' loving too. You the girl of my dreams, and I know you got some feelings for me too." He said slickly, hoping he had recited the lines as he had heard Smooth do on more than one occasion. Seeing that she was at a loss for words, he let his actions do the talking and pulled her closer. When he felt her settle against him, he knew that he finally had her. Within a two week time period, Darrell won her heart and stabbed out her virginity. Theirs would be an everlasting love…a gangsta love.

Chapter 6

Anger, relief disbelief, exhilaration, all tumbled in Dee Bastard's mind like a gyroscope gone wild. His mind wouldn't accept the fact that he was back locked up. He was rapidly sliding downhill. He sat in his 8 by 10 cell day in and day out wondering what LAPD really had on him? Unbeknown to the blind eye, Dee Bastard was batting a guilty conscious and the body counts he had on his hands were plentiful. There was Gunshot, the elder Crip gang member from his rival gang that was his first murder. Then, there were the snitches, Brother Bilal, Smooth, and Bo. Not counting the many murders that took place under his watch! However, Dee Bastard wasn't a killer. He was pushed and forced to execute. Anyone who became victim to his wrath deserved every bit of what they got.

"Man, stop tryna justify what you did," he told himself out loud. The three other inmates occupying the cell with Dee Bastard looked at each other and shook their heads. To them, Dee Bastard was a J-Cat (someone who lost his mind.) In jail, the most inmates cautioned themselves when a J-Cat was present because the bars and concrete walls are so strong, and the very existence of their physical presence become mental whereas most J-Cats

29

readily flip out. For lack of definition, in prison, even the strongest crack. And that was Dee Bastard until Bastard Child appeared at the bars of his cell.

"What's happening cuz!"

With broom in hand, BC had snuck into the cell block to check on his best friend. The two had been split up after being booked at Newton Police Station. And that was the problem! The two friends were booked together but were not charged with anything. BC figured it was just a violation of their terms and conditions of parole because two crime partners never reported to their parole officer upon their release. Still, there was some fishy stuff going on because neither Dee Bastard nor BC was informed that they were being violated. If anything the system was violating their Due Process Right. Law enforcement had 72 hours to arraign the pair on any charges brought against them. It had been five days since their recapture and they had heard no word about their situation. And due to the killing of the jailhouse rat the entire Los Angeles County Jail was on lockdown and the phones were turned off by higher officials. This made Dee Bastard wonder how and why was Bastard Child out of his cell. At this point, no one was to be trusted!

Dee Bastard looked up from his bunk and into the eyes of BC. Nothing looked strange to ever doubt his childhood friend. However, he could not seem to draw the strength to even say a word. He just stared at his comrade. "Damn nigga," BC said forever on his gangsta shit. "Shake that shit off cuz. What you stressed out? These muthafuckas got you going crazy or something."

Dee Bastard was mute. His mind was elsewhere. Where? No one knew not even him, Dee Bastard's cellmates all did gestures behind his back to signal to BC that Dee Bastard was a nut-case. They were doing everything in their power to let BC know Dee Bastard wasn't working with a full deck. Bastard Child caught a glimpse at one of the inmates and laughed "Ha!"

"Bastard, you even got these busta-ass niggaz in yo' cell thinking you a J-Cat. Cuz, you need to stop playing and get with the program."

"Hol' on Mexico who you callin' a busta? I'll beat the dog shit out of yo' Mexican-ass…"

Boom! Bang! Bing!

Before Bastard Child could reply or even stab the tough guy with his prison shank Dee Bastard leapt from his bunk and hit the guy with a left-right-left combination, knocking him completely out. "cuz you got the homie fucked up. Nigga, this still TLB or NOTHING. And you nothing!"

Just that fast BC had brought Dee Bastard from the grave. The beast had been awakened. This was the side of Dee Bastard everyone in his circle loved to see; especially his partner in crime BC.

"On Tiny Loc Bastardz, that's what I'm talking about. Fuck that bitch-ass nigga tryna sneak dis and shit." BC started Crip-Walking in front of the cell. To him and his Tupac syndrome, this was the life. It was ride or die. Crip or cry. TLB or NOTHING! He had to celebrate seeing Dee Bastard knock out the tough guy.

"Damn, cuz, I didn't think you had it in you no more," he admitted to Dee Bastard. "But I see you can't run from this Crippin' shit. Nahmean?"

Dee Bastard needed time to himself to clear his mind. He didn't want to be bothered with no one, not even Bastard Child. But Pedro knew how to get his friend to smile. He knew how to pump breath back into Dee Bastard's lifeless body.

"What up man? What do you want? I mean, damn, all our life every time you come around its trouble. One day, Imma really say to hell with all your nonsense."

Dee Bastard stepped over his cellmate who was still sleep on the concrete floor. The other two inmates started at him wide-eyed and terrified. They didn't know what to expect from the mentally disturbed Dee Bastard. "Don't worry I'm good. I'm not a J-Cat. Just going through some thangs." He told them.

The older cellmate with sprinkles of gray in his beard and head mumbled to himself "Thank you, Jesus. I didn't want to have to touch this youngsta."

Dee Bastard turned back to BC at the bars. "What up doe, Bastard?"

Dee Bastard whole demeanor changed. It was something about seeing someone that he knew. It uplifted his spirits and his state of depression had seemed to vanish with the wind. For sake of argument, he had adopted back to being incarcerated.

"Homie, I just had to sneak over here because homicide just came and got at me. Somebody is running they mouth. I told the fool we don't got nothing to talk about and if he gon book me, book me!"

Dee Bastard shook his head "Naw. But what did you tell them because a nigga starting to get paranoid about everything and everybody..."

"Wait! Wait!" Bastard Child frowned. "What you mean you getting paranoid about everything and everybody? What you tryna say?"

The tension between the two friends rose fast. It became so thick they shot each other a glare that only meant one thing: death. Needless to say but unspoken words are not unknown to the divine mind. Meaning one thing and one thing only: it was death before dishonor.

"Cuz, you talking out the side of your neck. This jailhouse shit got you really fucked up in the head. If I didn't know any better, I'd think you had flipped the script. Niggaz who run their mouth try to place blame on the next nigga and the way you been handling shit, I'm starting to second guess you!"

Dee Bastard swallowed spit. He wanted to hawk spit on Bastard Child for the first time in his life he felt betrayed by BC. However, this was divide and conquer at its finest; and the two young goons could not think pass got to collect their $200 and get out of jail free card.

"Youngstaz," Dee Bastard's old cellmate said. "I don't mean to be in yall business but I gotta tell yall these people love to divide and conquer. Once they get yall to break that's when they got a case. Until then they are fishing that's why they haven't charged yall with nothing. But best believe it's a weak link somewhere. So yall just keep your distance from each other and stay solid until the shit hit the fan. The Feds plant seeds so deep into organizations that you would have never expect. Learn from me. I been there before and the nigga who I did the shit with was the most solid nigga. He went to the grave with it."

Dee Bastard and BC never broke their combat stance. As the old head spoke truth into the situation, Dee Bastard thought back to old man Brother Ajene. Brother Ajene was a lifer who was well-respected and well-educated. He was the man who Dee Bastard credited for saving his life and opening his eyes to the destruction he did unto his people.

One day while in the cell, Brother Ajene told Dee Bastard "The difference between a wise man and a smart man is: The smart man learns from his own mistakes whereas the wise man learns from other people's mistakes. Be a wise man, not a smart one!"

Thinking back to what Brother Ajene had told him, Dee Bastard looked BC in the eyes and stated firmly. "Don't trip! I'll get to the bottom of this."

BC glared at his best friend and shook his head. He walked off hurt. He knew what Dee Bastard was thinking. They had been boys for many moons. The only question is, now who going to kill who first, BC thought as he crept back to his cell block.

The rules had only changed. There was no loyalty in the streets no more. Trust No One were the only words to describe the situation.

Chapter 7

"Hey, Laurell this is P. what's the latest on my boy Dee Bastard?" P had been calling Laurell day in and day out trying to get the 4-1-1 on Dee Bastard, but to his surprise, even Laurell hadn't heard from Dee Bastard. He was starting to wonder if BC and Dee Bastard were still alive. The jail was a mad house, and not only did they have to worry about the gang issues, they had to worry about the racial tension between blacks and Mexicans, the blacks and white boys, and the police, the latter being the deadliest gang throughout the system.

Laurell let out a breath of frustration through the phone. "No. I'm still waiting, P. I told you as soon as I hear from him, I will call you," Laurell said.

P could feel through the airwaves that Laurell was going through it. P knew Laurell carried the burden that it was her fault that Dee Bastard was back incarcerated. He knew Dee Bastard was supposed to been out the streets with them. If not with him, at least, with Laurell at home, moving slow, baby-making, and just enjoying freedom.

"Okay. My bad, sis. I didn't mean to bother you, he just been on my mind since I found out he was picked up."

P hung up with Laurell and turned toward Kioshi who was in the kitchen cooking. She stood naked as the day she was born. She stood over the stove flipping pancakes; her fat-round-yellow-ass sat on her back like a horse. P bit down on his bottom lip. He could see her fat pussy through the gap between her legs. It looked like a cameltoe and a Big Mac.

P slid up behind her and nibbled on her left ear as he whispered in it. "I wanna fuck you right now. Right here before we eat and go shopping."

Kioshi backed her ass into his crotch. That was the answer he needed. P slid out of his pants with the quickness and ushered Kioshi to the table a few feet over. He bent her over and she assisted him by spreading her legs. P gripped his rock hard dick and penetrated Kioshi from the back. Even though Kioshi got around and sold pussy to keep the bills paid, she had the best pussy ever to P. Every time he got inside Kioshi her pussy would lock on his dick like vise grips. The head of his dick swelled up so much that he had to slow down and learn how to control himself. If not, he would have been known as a one-minute-man to Kioshi because she had that fire!

Like a porn star, P fucked Kioshi from the back until he could see a puddle of her juice on the floor. The wetness dripped from her pussy onto his shaft, then down their legs. Kioshi moaned nonstop. One thing about P was he knew how to please her.

"Fuck me, Daddy!"

"Oh yes!"

"Fuck me!"

Kioshi arched her back as P dug deeper inside of her. Now his fingers were invading her ass. Kioshi went crazy. "Oh shit! Yes! Fuck me harder Percy."

Kioshi was a freak, a nympho. She cried out as P pounded her from the back like a wild animal. With her palms flat on the glass table, she gyrated her hips and backed her ass up. She looked over her shoulder as P went to work and she admired everything about him. From his athletic body to his short cut hairdo to his long 10-inch dick pumping in and out of her. Before she knew it her body started trembling and gave completely out. She fell to her knees.

"Damn, what happened? You alright?" P asked surprised.

"Yea. I am good. I slipped on the puddle of our fluids," she lied. The truth was P had fucked her so good she blanked out and her body got weak at the knees.

P shook his head. Kioshi had come a long way sexually. She wasn't the same shy girl whom he had taken her virginity. She was naughty, nasty, and uninhibited when it came to sex and P loved it.

"Put it in my mouth, Daddy."

P stood over her with his hands on his hips as Kioshi took him in her mouth. Kioshi head game was one many chicks needed to study. She was a professional boxer when it came to bobbing and weaving. Her head made most Johns go bankrupt.

She took every inch of P's 10-inch dick into her mouth. P grabbed the back of her head and forced his dick deeper down her throat. Kioshi thirsty for his protein went hard in the paint. She sucked, sucked, and sucked until the head of P's dick swelled up and he exploded in her mouth. She swallowed.

"Damn, this bitch got the coldest head game ever," P told himself.

"Well, I got my protein for the day. I'm not hungry no more. Can I have that money to go shopping now?"

"Just like a real whore, you give a nigga a blowjob then ask for some money," P joked. "You are the definition of a prostitute."

"Percy, be quiet. You know I love you. The other niggaz are just tricks. You are my future husband."

"Well, I can't tell," P said flopping on the couch in Kioshi's living room. "Well, let me tell you something. One, I don't cook for any of my clients. Two, none of them spends a night at my house. And three, I don't love any one of them. I love you."

P smiled inwardly. He knew he had a winner in Kioshi. He knew she was a keeper no matter what she did to pay the bills. "Okay cool. But look I need you to do two things for me. The first thing is to go to the projects meet up with my sister and Pooh. Keisha going to get me a rental I need you to take her the money. I gotta get low until I know what's good with Dee Bastard and BC. Second, I need you to keep your eyes and ears to the streets and find out what's going on with the TLB's and the power struggle over there. They say it's some new young niggaz who's tryna get on and you know when a nigga fear you or need you out the way they either going to tell on you or kill you. I think somebody took the coward way out with my boys."

Chapter 8

The Fox Hills Mall was crowded as usual on the weekend. Laurell and Kasey sat day in and day out waiting on Dee Bastard to call, but he never did. Together as a team, they called every police station and county jail in California. It was like Dee Bastard and BC were just taken off the planet earth and left on Mars because law enforcement wasn't giving up any information regarding their incarceration. Then, asked why they haven't received, at least, a courtesy call to call their family to advise them of their whereabouts. Laurell and Kasey were told because the whole county jail population is on lockdown. But the system was so corrupt, Dee Bastard and BC were supposed to receive their courtesy call at the arresting police station, not the county jail. Being a gangsta's girl wasn't easy at all; especially when the gangsta you love is behind bars. To clear her mind Laurell decided to go shopping. Every woman's therapy.

The Fox Hills Mall was lined with high-end stores, eateries, and jewelers. Laurell wanted to drop in H&M and Shiekh's for sure. She wanted to grab some candy from See's and stop at Hot Dog on a Stick. She loved their cherry lemonade. "Laurell!" Just as she made her way into the H&M someone

41

called her name. She stopped in mid-stride but didn't see anyone she knew. She was about to continue on into the store when someone called her name again. "Laurell!"

Out of nowhere Lil' Shawn and two of his boys came jogging up. Lil' Shawn was the new up-coming ghetto superstar in the hood. He had a crew of teeny-boppers under him that called themselves, The Tiny Mites. The Tiny Mites idolized the Tiny Loc Bastardz that's where the Tiny in the crew name came from. Just like the TLB's they were 4Trey Gangsta Crip recruits. The Tiny Mites were baby brothers of the TLB's. Lil' Shawn was the half brother of the late Dynasty. He even resembled and acted like Dynasty. The man who fathered the two goons held strong genes, because if one didn't know any better he or she would have thought they saw a ghost. One would have thought Dynasty was alive and whoever made the false rumor that he died from that car crash, lied.

"Dang, boy what's wrong with you," Laurell said seeing Lil' Shawn and his two puppets, Brandon and Mylo.

"Aww shit girl you know ain't nothing wrong," Lil' Shawn said holding up his shirt so Laurell and Kasey could see the butt of his .9mm. "A nigga will die in here fuckin' with me."

Lil' Shawn was a wild eighteen-year-old cat. He was fresh out of high school and felt he had a lot to prove. That coupled with trying to live up to his brother's legacy, he was a headache and accident waiting to happen.

Laurell shook her head. "Lil' Shawn, stop being dumb and pull your shirt down."

"And stop tryna act like your brother," Kasey added.

"Shut up, bitch! I ain't even talking to you. Talk when I give you permission to."

Laurell grabbed Kasey by the arm before the hot-headed Calliope Projects gangstress could reply. "Come on Kasey. Lil' Shawn, you are one rude-ass young nigga. Yo' young ass need to grow up."

Laurell started to walk off. Lil' Shawn grabbed her by the elbow. "Damn, Laurell, stop acting like you ain't feeling a young nigga. I know you like a young boss. Let me come over for dinner or something."

"Psst." Laurell snatched her arm loose. "Boy, if you don't take yo' young ass somewhere…"

"What you going to do?" Brandon chimed in. He was the younger brother of Rose and Lashonda. Laurell couldn't stand them for nothing in the world. Personally, she felt they had both slept with Dee Bastard, even though he and Rose only claimed to be best friends. And Lashonda was community pussy.

"Brandon, you know I don't like you, your sisters or anyone in your household, so you need to take your fat ass somewhere and get out my face." Laurell turned back to Lil' Shawn. "Now Shawn don't ever get at me like that. You know who my man is and how tight he and your brother was. Everybody know you want to be like your brother, but boo-boo you are nothing like him, and I pray you wise up because Don would have never tried to holla at me."

Lil' Shawn resembled the rapper T.I.P and the Devil. His skin tone was copper brown, but when he became angry it turned beet red. He frowned. "Bitch, you don't know what you talking about. I was just tryna give yo' dumb ass a chance to get on the winning team because it seems like your loser-ass boyfriend can't stay out of jail."

Laurell couldn't come to terms of why she even wasted another minute standing there going back and forth with Lil' Shawn. He was a complete fool and bonehead. "Little boy, you need to grow up. I will never be on your team. That's like the blind leading the blind. And so speaking of my husband, your whole crew idolize him. But I guess like Lil' Kim say 'the same people idolize you criticize you'. So it doesn't surprise me that you are jealous and want what my man got."

Laurell walked off leaving Lil' Shawn and his boys high and dry. "Bitch, fuck you and yo' man!" Lil' Shawn shouted behind her. "This Tiny Mites or NOTHING!"

Laurell ignored Lil' Shawn and his puppets, but for the rest of the day, she was be bothered by some of the things Lil' Shawn said. She knew a lot of cats envied Dee Bastard, but she didn't know to what extent. Even the youngster's on the block held hatred for Dee Bastard from jealousy a mile long.

After a long day of shopping and being out, Laurell lay in bed thinking about her day. Not only did the incident with Lil' Shawn bothered her, but she thought back to the dressing room of H&M. Laurell tried on garment after garment. She found herself parading in front of the mirror back and forth. Kasey moved in behind her and closed the dressing room door. She ran her hand across the Gucci romper Laurell had on. Her nipples stood at attention as Kasey touched them. "Can I eat your pussy right here, right now in front of this mirror?"

Laurell slightly shoved her ass into Kasey. "Kasey, please don't do that in this store. They might got hidden cameras."

Even though, Laurell didn't allow Kasey to lick between her legs doesn't mean the thought didn't cross her mind as Kasey kneaded her breast and began grinding her ass and kissing the nape of her neck. Kasey reached between her legs and dug her fingers into Laurell's wet pussy. "Now, tell me you don't like what I'm doing and I will stop."

Laurell warm love juices soaked Kasey's fingers and ran down her thighs. There was no way Laurell could deny the pleasure Kasey was giving her. The truth of the matter was, she was deprived sexually due to Dee Bastard being gone seven long years to only return home for a few days. Laurell suppressed the moans that escaped her mouth. She was just about to give in to Kasey's magic touch when two knocks came at the dressing room door.

"Is you guys okay in there?"

It was the dressing room employee.

"Here we come right now," Kasey said.

Laurell removed Kasey's fingers from her womb and slid them into her mouth. After removing Kasey's fingers from her mouth, she asked Kasey "Is there something different about me?"

"I don't know. Maybe I'm tripping, but it looks like you getting fat..."

Laurell lay in bed looking at the ceiling in deep thought. Kasey was once again beside her sleep. She had been fallen asleep feeling neglected. Lately, since Dee Bastard's recapture, Kasey could not get any affection. Now with the thought of her possibly being pregnant things were destined to get worse.

Tears rolled out Laurell's eyes and down her cheeks. She was consumed by her thoughts. She had always dreamed of having kids and a family with Dee Bastard. He had been and was the only man she ever loved. However, motherhood was a different stage of life. She knew without confirmation that she was pregnant. Her body was changing. Despite all the vomiting, she just felt it. "But damn why now?" she asked herself. "I could hold him down during his time, but shit gonna be 100 times harder with a baby. Damn, what am I to do? Dee Bastard, I need you to call. I need you home. I need to know something".

Laurell cried herself to sleep. Dee Bastard had left her once again. All lonely and by herself.

Chapter 9

"Man, these kids nowadays can't never be on time." Big Wrap waited impatiently at the entrance of Friday's in the Marina. He glanced around occasionally looking for Shady. "The nigga said to be here at eight on the dot and it's going on eight-thirty. Black folks always a day late and a dollar short."

As Big Wrap thought out loud to himself a fine sista with honey-colored hair that complimented her skin tone walked out of the restaurant. She was gorgeous and had a banging body. She strutted passed him demanding attention.

Her fat round ass shifted its weight from left to right.

Damn, this is one bad bitch. My dick is hard just looking at her. And she don't look like no hood bitch. I bet she's a lawyer or something.

Big Wrap took a few steps forward cutting her off. "Excuse me beautiful, I was wondering why such a beautiful sista as yourself is walking out of this restaurant by yourself?"

The woman smiled flashing her pearly whites. She looked over her shoulders pointing with her eyes back into Friday's. "I am here with that guy seated at the bar awaiting your entrance."

Shady sat at the bar smiling. Big Wrap had surveilled the whole perimeter upon his arrival. This was part of his survival tactic being a veteran gang member in the streets of Los Angeles. However, Shady name was his character.

It fit him to a T. He stayed camouflaged and in the shade of things.

Big Wrap extended his hand to the beautiful woman and smiled. She extended hers back. He kissed the back of her hand and introduced himself. "BW. And your name is?"

"Zoe Miller."

Zoe turned and pointed to Shady with her head. "He's waiting for you." She continued her journey.

Big Wrap made his way into Fridays and found a seat at the bar next to Shady. "What it look like captain," Wrap greeted.

The OG and YG exchanged daps. Shady got straight to the point. "When the last time you seen BT?"

The puzzled look grew on Wrap's face. "He was just at the shop last night before he went to

49

meet up with that white bitch that came with that broad Trapstar had with him the night of the party. Why? What's up?"

Shady shook his head slowly contemplating how to drop the bomb on Wrap. "Okay. Check this out. Last night, I went to check on Momma Mary and grab a plate. When I was leaving that white detective who's always on the news and the one they say twisted Killa Black, drove by creeping in a Caprice. The police kind. I stood in the cut whereas I couldn't be seen and watched the car go by. Inside, was BT pointing at Momma Mary's house…"

Big Wrap couldn't believe his ears. BT was part of his tight-knit circle. His crew called themselves The Third Place. They were all older 4 Trey's who Big Wrap ran. He was the undisputed leader no doubt and he could not digest the thought that one of his boys was seen in a police car pointing things out. He had known BT his whole life. He knew Shady eyes may have deceived him. "You sure it was BT?" Wrap asked hoping Shady would say he was not sure.

Shady nodded his head. "I knew you were going to doubt me, but just know, there are snakes in the garden and we gotta clean them out before we all end up under the jail."

As much as Wrap wanted his lil' nigga to be misinformed about seeing BT working with the police, he knew Shady was a stand up young gangsta and general of the TLB's. He tried to give BT the benefit of doubt, but Shady had no reason to lie on BT. the two had a fair bond and Shady was known to respect his elders.

"Man, this shit is getting worse by the day. This is so watered down out here we all going to drown if we don't leave the life we live alone," Big Wrap said. "And I say that to say this…"

Wrap paused thinking over his next words. "Baby boy, I might be stubborn by nature, but I'm far from dumb. As painful as it might be, momma said my heart will never lead me wrong or fail me. And I feel in my heart of hearts that you are the last of a dying breed and my lil' nigga who I would always go to bat for. So I believe you…"

"Would you guys like some drinks?" the waitress interrupted.

Shady looked at Wrap. "What you drinking? It's on me."

Wrap turned to the young college student waitress and said "Bring me a double shot of Hennessy. NO Ice."

Shady slid the waitress a crisp hundred dollar bill and said "I'll have the same thing. And that's your tip. I'll cover the tab later/"

The waitress smiled and walked off. She was happier than a child on Christmas.

"I see you smooth with the ladies," Wrap informed. "I take it you did learn something from the old man huh?"

Wrap popped his collar. But who was that fine sista, Zoe Miller? Where she come from because we all know she's not a product of our environment."

A snide grin stretched across Shady's face. "She's fine as wine huh?"

Wrap furred his brows up and down in agreement.

Well, she's the lawyer handling all my moms' stuff. Like she just got the life insurance check cleared. You know they tried to prolong the process, but she made it happen."

"So what you gonna do with the money?"

Shady gave the question a brief thought and said: "I'm gonna fix the house momma left me and make sure we on the same page."

"That's not a bad plan," Wrap informed. "But back to BT. Do you feel his plug need to be pulled or not?"

The waitress brought back their drinks and the two Crips indulged. They threw the fiery liquor back like it was water and wiped their lips with the back of their palms in unison. Shady looked at the waitress who was digging his swag and blushing like a shy school girl with a crush. He told her "Keep 'em coming."

With all the snitching going on in the hood, they needed something to ease the pain. They knew with the pigs adding another snake into the garden, things were going to get hectic. It was just a matter of time and the question was when?

"Real talk, you know as much as I'm known for being a solid nigga, I ain't with the 1-8-7, but I'm gonna have to do something and do it quick! I lost my mom's to this shit so I'm damn sho aint bout to lose any more of my folks. We gon have to do whatever seems fit. I mean, no body, no murder right?"

Big Wrap couldn't do anything but smile. They didn't make young cats like Shady anymore. Not only was he street smart, he was book smart too. He displayed his maturity in every situation no matter what it was. Shady should have been somewhere high up in the mountains, living a successful life, but instead, he was stuck at the bottom being loyal to people whom in turn were proven to be disloyal by the day.

"If I didn't understand your struggle, I would call you the biggest fool I know. The reason you outshine all the other TLB's and the only one who's from yall original clique who is not dead or in jail is because you are ten times smarter than you put on. You and Dee Bastard's downfall is y'all loyalty to the hood. Being loyal to this shit only lead to two places. Pick your poison or get that money from your mom's life insurance and move on."

"That's the realist shit ever. That's exactly what I needed to hear. Wrap you are a real big homie. I love you for that. Let's get together more often like this because I really be needing the words of encouragement."

Wrap patted Shady on the back as he stood up to leave. "Now what you need is a good woman on your side to motivate you. One who wants the best for you. If I was you, I will go after Zoe Miller. I could tell she's digging you. She might have you by a few years but she like something about you. Mark my words. But anyhow, when you get up and going tomorrow come by GMA, I got something for you."

GMA, which stood for Gangstaz Moving Appliances, was Big Wrap's store that he visioned to be the next Radio Shack or Best Buy for hood people. In the back of the store; in his office, Wrap was known to conduct all his personal or business meetings there, so he even surprised himself

54

agreeing to meet Shady at Friday's in the Marina. However, it was fun while it lasted, but it was time for him to get back to his comfort zone. The two gangsters: young and old, exchanged handshakes and parted ways.

Chapter 10

The next day after BC had snuck to Dee Bastard's cell and told him that homicide had come to talk to him, Dee Bastard was called out of his cell for a conference in the attorney room. Beads of sweat crowded his forehead from the many thoughts that crossed his mind. 'What's this?' he thought. 'I hope it's just the parole board letting me know what's good with my situation. But damn, how shit been going, I hope it's not an attorney talking about he's here to represent me in a murder case. That will be my nightmare come true. Then, again, it could be the same people who BC was tryna tell me about before I snapped on him'.

As Dee Bastard was shackled around the wrist and ankles, he thought of every possibility. He was then escorted from his cell block, down a long stretch of hallway to the attorney room. The deputy closed the door after he was shoved inside. The door made a loud thud sound. The room was dark. So dark Dee Bastard had to close his eyes and open them again. His gut feeling told him something was not right about the situation. The atmosphere was something he had only seen in movies: when the bad guy was about to get brutally beat and interrogated. And that's just what happened to Dee

Bastard. Once his eyes adjusted to the darkness, Dee Bastard spotted the white detective he had seen numerous of times on television, standing in the center of the room with a thick folder in his hand. "Mr. Davis," he said kicking an empty chair toward Dee Bastard. "Take a seat."

Silence. Dee Bastard didn't budge.

"Ooh, so we going to play the hardcore role huh, Mr. Davis? Or better yet, Mr. Dee Bastard. The legendary founder of the big bad TLB crew."

Silence. Dee Bastard was not a rookie. He knew to stay quiet doing this engagement. He knew the people only use what you tell them against you.

To calm his own nerves, Detective Gilmore lit a cigarette for himself. He did not like this one bit. This was something he did for the suspects once he had them on the edge of breaking. He needed Dee Bastard to make his case other than the little information he was able to squeeze out of the whore and BT wasn't enough to stand on during a trial. Detective Gilmore had to come up with a plan fast if he wanted that fifteen minutes of fame again.

After he lit the cigarette he offered Dee Bastard one. "Here take this. It will ease the situation. I know they haven't been treating you right back there."

Silence filled the room again. Dee Bastard held steady. Eyeing Gilmore, he began to think back to the murders of Bo and Smooth, then the shootout at the club, then the threesome with Laurell and Kasey, then all the years he spent locked in a cage. Dee Bastard thought back to how he lost everything to the streets; how his whole crew was eradicated by the police or buried six feet deep. He thought about Laurell and how she told him it's hard being a faithful, loyal woman to a man in jail. He thought of his mother and how he didn't even see Mary for one minute while he was out. Everything played in slow motion in Dee Bastard's head. Like a movie on rewind, this was the moment of truth.

"Okay Mr. Dee Bastard, this my last chance at giving you the opportunity to save your own ass, because you might know I already know you killed Bo and Smooth. I also know you killed that Muslim snitch in prison. I know everything. I even know you might have a successful career as an author and publisher if you ever could get back out of here. But!"

Gilmore paused to let the word "But" linger. BUT! Leave it up to Mr. Pedro Guzman aka Bastard Child. You are a serial killer who needs to be put down by the needle or locked in prison for the rest of your natural life."

Dee Bastard stood still. He knew Gilmore had done this type of work many times; it was his job to solve crimes and recover information. Even though Gilmore's tone of voice conveyed the seriousness of the situation of murder, life behind the walls, and the death penalty, Dee Bastard was part of the ten percent crew, he wasn't about to tell Gilmore anything. He served him with a piece of cake called the "Silent Treatment".

Gilmore stood smoking the Newport to the yellow. He blew the smoke directly into Dee Bastard's face. If the young gangsta wasn't shackled at his waist and ankles he would have punched the corrupt cop in his snot box. Dee Bastard may have been losing his mind from feeling so hopeless, but one thing he told himself was he wasn't about to lose his dignity. He stood at attention like he was in the military being drilled by a drill sergeant. He closed his eyes and thought about his new book.

CRACK!

As his eyes were closed Gilmore pulled out a solid steel baton from his side waist and cracked Dee Bastard over the back. Then, a straight jab of the stick to his stomach. Dee Bastard fell to his knees. Pain shoot through his body but he still didn't say a word. He told himself *I'd rather get beat like a runaway slave right now than spend the rest of my life in modern-day slavery.*

The pain Gilmore delivered was unbearable to most. With tactics like these Dee Bastard could see how ninety percent of the so-called thugs, gangsters, and hustlers go from good to bad overnight. With no time to react to the vicious beating, Dee Bastard curled up in a ball on the floor. Still shackled he could do nothing but blank out. Gilmore swung the steel baton like a slave owner beating a recaptured slave. Before each blow of the steel, you heard whooshing sounds through the air. And each blow would crack, break, or shatter a bone.

Dee Bastard thought he was dead until he heard the muffled sound of Gilmore's voice. "You might get away this time, but from now on I'm on your ass like a fly on shit…"

CRACK!

Chapter 11

Laurell had tossed and turned all night. For some reason, she could not sleep. She got out of bed and ran directly to the bathroom. She made it in time enough to bury her face in the toilet bowl and vomit. The pains in her stomach would not stop coming. She couldn't avoid the obvious. She was pregnant and going through the symptoms was stressful.

"Yea you pregnant," Kasey emerged at the bathroom door. She wiped the sleep from her eyes and continued. "So come on and get dressed. We going to the hospital!"

Laurell's heart rate slowed. She was scared of the news she was destined to receive. She bolted upright. The pain had vanished. "I'm okay. I think I ate something I wasn't supposed to."

"Stop it, Rell. Girl, you are pregnant and we both know it."

"Kasey, it's only been a few weeks since Darrell put his thing in me. I am not prego."

Kasey waved Laurell off. "Okay, play mind games with yourself. I'm going back to bed. If you need me call me and I'll come running."

For the next hour, Laurell stood over the bowl. The sperm had sprouted the seed and the transformation of life was stirring up a lot of commotion in her stomach. Laurell told herself 'Shit if I gotta deal with this for nine months, I might have to consider abortion'.

Just as the pain ceased, Laurell decided to call it a night.

The next morning, Laurell woke up to the smell of breakfast: pancakes, eggs, bacon, grits, and orange juice. Kasey had been up cooking for the past two hours. She glanced into the room and saw Laurell was awake and brought her a plate. "Here you go, baby. Hope you feel better.'"

"I do," Laurell informed.

"Okay. Cool," Kasey said kissing her on the lips then forehead. "I'm bout to head to the store to get a few items and a pregnancy test. Do you want anything?"

"No I'm good, but yes please get that pregnancy test for me; because I wanna know my damn self."

After Kasey left and Laurell threw back the breakfast, she decided to write Dee Bastard and check online to see if they updated their system. She was determined to locate Darrell this day, even if it meant walking into the chief of police and the parole office demanding answers. *Damn, just thinking about it that's what I should have been doing! My man could be dead for all I know.*

Laurell became heated at herself. 'What real woman does that? Let her nigga, sit in jail for weeks before she tries to find him. I need my ass whipped'.

She got straight to the letter:

Dear Darrell,

I hope and pray you are alright. I don't know what your situation is because these people not giving up any information regarding you or BC. I'm fed up with myself because as your better half, I feel I suppose to have been heard from you or figured out your whereabouts and what you are up against. But today I'm going all in! I'm going to the chief of police and the parole office if I don't hear nothing from you today!

Anyhow, Darrell, I have been feeling really sick lately. I don't know how to tell you, but I think I'm pregnant. I have been throwing up and my period has yet to come. Kasey just went to grab a pregnancy test for me. But I want to know your true feelings if I am prego? I mean, we both got to get our shit together and grow up but I will save that conversation for the next letter. As of right now I just need to know you are alright. Today, I'm demanding answers…

Missing you like crazy!

Love Always Your Wifey

Laurell Davis

Riiiiinnng!

Riiiiinnng!

Just as Laurell finished writing the letter her house phone started to ring. She knew and figured it to be Dee Bastard because the house phone barely rang. Everyone knew to call her cell phone. Basically, the house phone was for emergency use only.

Laurell leapt from the table where she was seated writing and beelined to the house phone. She answered on the second ring. "Hello!"

"Rell, why you not answering your cell phone?"

It was Laurie

"Because it never rang!" Laurell would later find out that somehow she had accidentally turned the ringer off on her cell phone. She shook her head. 'Damn, what if Darrell been calling and my dumb-ass been having the phone on silent the whole time'.

"Anyways, I talked to BC just now and he said him and Dee got into it because Dee is losing his mind. He said shit been looking bad for them. First, homicide pulled him out the cell talking about some shit he said he knew nothing about. He said they knew some shit and tried to make it like Dee told…"

"What my man ain't never no snitch!"

"Damn, Rell, would you let me finish?"

"SMACK!" Laurell smacked her lips not trying not to hear nothing else her sister had to say. People talked bad about God, but they weren't going to talk bad about her future husband. "Go on ahead. Finish what you were saying."

"Well, he said after they tried to twist him and say Dee told on him, he stuck to the script and the detective hit him over the head with a billy club. He said he got saved when an attorney walked into the wrong room and said "hey!"

Laurell was now heated. She hadn't heard from Dee Bastard but she knew it was two sides to each story. *Who Mexican-ass BC think he is, tryna throw salt on my nigga name like that. He the one probably snitching. Shit, why no one heard from my husband?*

"He also told me after the detective walked out of the room, he snuck down the hallway to Dee's cell and when he got there Dee was acting weird…"

"Look, Rell, don't be getting mad at me. I'm just telling you what was told to me."

"Okay. Just hurry up and finish because I'm not buying anything BC is saying."

"Well, he said Dee been acting weird like he losing his mind. Like he stressed out. He says he ain't the same…"

"Ain't the same like how?" Laurell snapped. "What, because he probably ain't running around tryna get in more trouble like his Mexican-ass?"

"I don't know, but he said, when he told Dee what had just gone down with the police, Dee flipped out. They exchanged words and he walked off. They haven't spoke or seen each other since. But he says he saw the parole board today and he only got a violation…"

"Well, Imma call you later because I still haven't talked to Darrell. And now I'm wondering how the fuck do BC only got a violation if the police talking hot ones?"

CLICK!

Laurell hung up before her twin could reply. It was some strange weeds growing in the garden. A lot of suspect activity was taking place. It was like being in a pool full of piranhas. Laurell ran to her cell phone and checked her missed call log to make sure Dee Bastard had not called. She only had one missed call and that was from Shady.

Chapter 12

"Damn, what happened to you homie," Shady asked Dee Bastard as Dee Bastard wheeled himself behind the glass in the visiting area of the Los Angeles County Jail.

"Man," Dee Bastard replied shaking his head. He was embarrassed. He knew Shady was one of his most loyal homeboys, but he hated for his childhood friend to see him in such bad condition. Ironically, Shady had perfect timing because ten minutes earlier Dee Bastard just been released from the medical module hole. The pigs kept him isolated from the general population until some of the bruises and swelling went down from Detective Gilmore's beating. The sad part about the situation, Dee Bastard had to learn firsthand how the system all work together. While sitting up with his body aching full of pain 24/7, having nightmares and flashbacks of Gilmore coming back to get him, he had many hours to think, relax his mind, and figure out his situation. They say that God works in mysterious ways and gives a lot of blessings in disguise.

Dee Bastard kind of felt the beating he received was a blessing from God because it woke him up from the dead. Before the showdown with Detective Gilmore and the fallout with BC, he could not count to five from one. His mind and better judgment were that clouded. What he failed to realize, better yet forgot, was that jail is more mental than physical. To survive incarceration an inmate must submit the body but they can't take the mind unless one lets them.

After coming back to his senses, Dee Bastard figured out the hoax. Butch killing the rat was all set up by the deputies to lock down the jail whereas Dee Bastard nor BC could communicate to each other or the outside world. This way Gilmore protected his case and informants. Also, this locked down all their systems and shut down visits. With these services not functioning, it bought Gilmore more time and an empty attorney room where he could interrogate and beat Dee Bastard and BC into admitting the murders or at least recover information he could use against them. And only after failed attempts, would he then beat them half to death to buy more time while they lay unconscious in the infirmary. Adding insult to injury, the deputies would write the injury incident reports up as if Dee Bastard tried to assault a deputy while resisting.

"So damn, that's what happened?" Shady shook his head as tears filled his eyes. He hated seeing his friends go through such treatment; especially how Gilmore tried to divide and conquer.

Shady was no punk but he was not stupid either. He knew jail wasn't for him that's why he stayed out of the way in his own lane. Shady was a wise man. He learned from his friends' mistakes.

Dee Bastard nodded with two black eyes and a broken collar bone. "straight like that homie. They tryna really build a case out of nothing."

Shady forced a smile. Even weak, full of pain, and beat up real bad, his friend knew how to make light of all situations. This what made Shady believe in Dee Bastard and his gift of storytelling. Despite his adversity and struggles to stay out of prison, Dee Bastard was very articulate, smart, strong, persuasive, and even argumentative. This was how the founder of the notorious Tiny Loc Bastardz came up with an empire of soldiers.

Gathering his thoughts, Shady said "Alright. Look I'm glad you told me everything because I brought my lawyer with me because we handling some shit with my mom's assets and as I promised you before you got locked back up, Imma fuck with you on your book business and dreams. Also, on the street side of things, everything gonna get taken care of. They boy BT…"

Shady paused and shook his head letting Dee Bastard know BT was the informant. He didn't want to say much through the glass, but Dee Bastard caught on quick.

Dee Bastard stared deep into Shady's eyes and knew the sincerity in his glare. He could not believe after all the years BT had put in being a standup guy, how could he go out backward. 'I guess they say living the gangsta life doesn't come with a 401k plan huh?' He shook his head with his hands in his palms and at that very moment, it dawned on him.

"Oh, shit!" he spoke, breaking the silence. "For a minute, these muhfuckaz had me all fucked up in the head. I thought it was BC or two of my goons. But I need you to hit Laurell and tell her to get in contact with my kid out of the projects. She gonna know who I'm talking about. Tell her to tell him to make sure yellow bone ain't doing nothing with white girl because if I recall right, sour candy was hollering at whitey when Twin walked off. You know how shit spread and niggaz and bitches pillow talk."

Shady nodded in agreement. "Will do."

"Also, bruh, before I signal my lawyer over here I wanna talk to you about some real shit. You know how I lost my mom, right?"

"True that," Dee Bastard replied, not knowing where Shady was going with the conversation.

"Well, homie, let me tell you are wrong…"

Shady paused letting his words sink in. "Nigga, you wrong as two left shoes. Cuzz, you only get one mom! Why you didn't go visit her homie?" You know that shit ain't cool. I'm not trying to put you down my nigga but sometimes we all need a little tough love and chastising."

"My nigga," Dee Bastard started to explain. "Shit happened so fast. A lot of shit happened that wasn't supposed to happen. It seems like everything that could have gone wrong, went wrong!"

Shady nodded. "But my boy, when you get out, make sure Momma Mary be the first person you see because I know she bout to be the first person you call when you get to use the phone. And when you call her, make sure you really talk to her nah mean?"

Shady wanted to tell Dee Bastard about the heart attack Mary suffered, but he felt it wasn't the time nor the place to do it. He figured it would have been less stress if Mary told him over the phone while letting him know she was alright.

"I hear you loud and proud, bruh. I'ma right my wrongs."

"Okay cool, now back to the book business. My moms use to always tell me whatever I do in life, give it my all, put the pedal to the metal and go all gas no brakes. Homie, I believe in you and your talent. You are the only nigga I know that wrote a book , so let's make this shit work. I was thinking we should start a publishing company called NBP

(No Brakes Publishing) and a record label called Triple Money Inc..."

Shady paused and signaled his lawyer. Zoe Miller came prancing toward the window. She stood behind Shady with her palms on his shoulders. "Dee this is Zoe Miller. Zoe Miller this is Darrell Davis."

The two nodded at each other.

"Dee, Zoe is here to help us get the publishing company started. She's going to ask you a few questions and we going to take it from there."

Dee Bastard looked at his comrade and couldn't do anything but smile. It felt damn good to know someone else other than himself believed in his craft and could see his vision. Life was still a roller coaster for this young redeeming gangsta. He told him "Shit was good a few weeks ago. Then, a nigga hit rock bottom again. Now, seem like better days are looming. This is the life of a TLB!"

Chapter 13

"Yeah, what's my name?!"

"What's my name?"

"Oooough. Big Daddy Shawn," the young curvy, slim big booty cutie from around the way said.

"Say it again. What's my name

What's my name?"

Lashonda faked another orgasm. "Oooough, shit. Yes!"

"Big Daddy Shawn!"

Lil' Shawn had Lashonda bent over touching her toes. He was knocking the lining out of her pussy from the back, giving Lashonda his all. In which to Lashonda was nothing. *Lil' Shawn young ass do not know what he's doing, but if he gonna be the next HNIC I got to play my role.*

Lil' Shawn was too young and too naïve to know Lashonda's past because if he did, he would have known that Lashonda was the biggest slut, slash snake the hood had ever seen. Not only did she manage to have slept with Bastard Child and

Bo, but also his brother. She was part cause of his brother's death. See, if Lil' Shawn knew half the things the streets knew, he would have been a better street thug. But since he lacked street knowledge he was bound to drown.

"Come for me baby," Lashonda said wanting this to end. Lil' Shawn sex grade was an F. She laughed inwardly at this little boy who thought he was a man. *Lil' nigga so dumb I'ma rob him dry just like I did his brother. I guess, being suckaz for love run in their bloodline.*

Riiiiinnng!

Riiiiinnng!

Just as Lil' Shawn was about to climax his cell phone started to go off nonstop. He glanced over to the nightstand and looked at the screen. It read: BT.

Oh shit! That's the big homie. Gotta see what he want, he told himself. He suddenly pulled out of Lashonda and grabbed his cell phone. "What up big homie? What's good?"

Lashonda mumbled "thank you Jesus" as he took the call. Lil' Shawn was horrible with his five-inch dick.

"Where you at homie? We need to talk?" BT stated on the other end of the phone.

74

"I'm wherever I need to be big homie. Just let me know when and where. You know the Tiny Mites down for the cause."

BT knew Lil' Shawn was a toy soldier compared to his brother. Dynasty, aka Bastard Don, would have never jumped so easily. It even made BT think back to the time Don stormed out of Big Wrap's office after telling Big Wrap "Fuck You. This TLB or NOTHING!" To Don, gangbanging wasn't about making friends, it was about making enemies. And BT felt he needed to put this in Lil' Shawn's head to stir up a little more heat in the hood to get the heat that was brewing his way off of him. He knew he couldn't do anything in the dark and expect it not to come to light. After deciding to turn informant he knew the risk he faced.

"Meet me in the parking lot of the shopping center on Slauson and Western in front of the Shoe Millennium. Be there in thirty minutes."

"Okay. Cool. I'm there."

Click!

Lil Shawn hung up, removed the condom from his now limp dick and looked at Lashonda. "Get dressed and get out."

Lashonda narrowed her eyes at him. "Ooh, so you just gonna fuck me and throw me out?!" She faked an attitude, Getting put out was nothing new to her, but she had to make a point. "See that's why I don't fuck with young niggaz like you."

"Bitch shut up and get out," Lil' Shawn snapped as he grabbed her panties, sweatpants, T-shirt, and tossed them at her. "Hurry up! I gotta go handle somebody with the big homie."

"Lil' Shawn you are a joke. Give me a minute and I'll be out this rat and roach infested ass house."

Lashonda sat up slid on her clothes and pushed Lil' Shawn out of her way. "And you so dumb you got the whole hood in your hands, but still living with your mom and doing whatever yo' so-called big homies tell you to do. Be your own man."

Lashanda wanted to crush his spirits just as he tried to crush hers. At first, she was going to tell him how weak his sex was but figured it was best to play on his other weakness.

"Bitch, I'm Lil' Shawn! Everybody respect my gangsta. I am my own man. I do what the fuck I want! Bitch this Tiny Mites or NOTHING! And niggaz know."

Lashonda walked out of the bedroom to the front door, he went in on her. "Bitch you know I'm the shit that's why you just bent that fat ass over for me. Second, how you gon' talk about my mom's house when your pussy smells like shit. I had to cover my nose while I was fucking. Yo' titties are

76

lop-sided. One look like an apple; the other look like a cantaloupe. And your breath smells like hot ass and corn grease. That's why I didn't want no head and I'm kickin' yo' weak ass out. You're dismissed!"

Lil' Shawn opened the door for her and Lashonda walked out with a cheesy smile on her face. Despite the verbal lashing, she was sure Lil' Shawn would be hitting her up for more.

$$$

Lil' Shawn pulled into the darkened parking lot and found BT parked in his new BMW 528i puffing on a Newport. It was a quarter past ten so the shopping center was empty. The only other cars entering the parking lot was the ones headed to the 24 hour McDonald's on the other end of the lot. Lil' Shawn parked his Challenger next to the passenger door of BT's BMW. He leapt from his car and hopped in with BT. His heart was pounding anticipating what BT had to talk to him about. He knew BT was part of the infamous Third Place clique. With BT, Big Wrap and a few other reputable 4 Trey's at the helm of the crew, Lil' Shawn figured it was important to keep them as allies. This is what helped the Tiny Loc Bastardz become known and respected in the streets of Los Angeles and he wanted to follow the lead. Well, until he felt it was time to blow up on everybody. He'd heard his brother did the same thing.

"What's good youngsta?" BT asked as Shawn closed the car door. They exchanged daps.

"Shit you tell me," Lil' Shawn replied.

"A whole lot that could equal to whole of nothing if we get to it fast enough."

"What you talking about?" Lil' Shawn had a puzzled look on his face.

BT spoke in riddles that were over the young goons' head. "Well, peep game. It was brought to my attention that the TLB, and my crew, don't want the Tiny Mites to exist anymore…"

Lil' Shawn instantly became heated. "What?!" His pride, ego, and everything concerning his machoism were tampered with. He looked up to the TLB's but how could they be plotting the Tiny Mites demise?

"Yeah man I was at GMA today and my clique was saying the TLB's feel it shouldn't be no more cliques within the 4 Trey's after them…"

"Wait. Wait," Lil' Shawn cut BT off. "Who is them because truthfully it ain't that many TLB's no more and Dee Bastard and BC back in jail so who you talking about?"

BT had his plan mapped out. He said "See, you got Shady. He's they main man right now. And let me tell you about that nigga…"

BT paused thinking about the night he took Gilmore by Momma Mary's house to point Shady out to Gilmore. The detective wanted to know who was the driver that dropped Dee Bastard and BC off at Laurell's apartment the day they got booked. BT overheard Shady tell Big Wrap that he dropped the pair off after the murders were carried out. However, after extensive background searches on Shady nothing came up. This Shady guy was clean as a whistle and from surveillance, he was dating a well known civil attorney who was on the senior board of top law firm Jay Cooper and Company. Gilmore decided not to pursue Shady even though he associated with a lot of criminal-minded individuals.

As BT thought of Shady he wondered did the young general see him in the car with the detective? From the angle he sat inside the car he figured, he went unseen but just for insurance on his life he had to put a double cross into play. BT had nothing to lose. He had already sold his soul to the devil.

Man, they don't call white people blue-eyed devils for nothing, he told himself. *Not only did that white bitch Charlotte set me up so did that punk-ass detective.*

"Damn, homie are you going to finish telling me or you just going to go quiet on a nigga?" Lil' Shawn said knocking BT out of thought.

"Oh yeah! My bad. I was just thinking about how much dirt Shady put in and how many soldiers he still got behind him." BT ran both hands through his hair to make his lies genuine.

"Plus, the reason I'm telling you this because as much shit as your big brother stirred up he was my only real little homie. I was the one who told him Bo and 'em other niggaz had a hit out on him. I'm the one who supplied him with guns when he went to war. Even when he went on the run, I was the one paying for all that. All these other niggaz didn't care about my nigga Don like I did because that was my real little homie. He went to the grave with a lot of shit we done. He kept it 'G'."

BT would have been a great novelist. His storytelling was of the greats. He knew how to build a climax and an explosive ending. Lil' Shawn was planted to his seat like a student studying the professor.

"So to make a long story short, for the sake of Bastard Don I'm going against the grain telling you this information because they supposed to be doing a sneak attack on yall soon…"

Lil' Shawn's eyes widened. "When?"

BT shrugged his shoulders. "Nigga, if I knew I'll tell you. But my only thing is you and your crew gotta suit up and hit the TLB's first."

"I dig." Lil' Shawn nodded in agreement.

"My only thing is you gotta keep me out of it. Go to your grave with what I'm telling you. Even when you explain the situation to your crew don't mention my name. You feel me?"

"Got you."

The two pounded each other on the fist and parted ways.

Chapter 14

"Laurell, what do you want, child? You know I'm mad at you and that man of yours," Mary told Laurell as she walked into Mary's house.

Laurell tilted her head to the floor from a guilty conscious. "Momma Mary, I went to see Darrell. It's been almost four weeks since I have seen or heard from him. But to be honest with you that's not why I'm here."

The two women proceeded to the couches in the living room. Laurell looked at a picture of her and Darrell from their junior high school days. Her eyes became blurry from the unshed tears mounting ready to fall rapidly down her cheeks.

"Momma, to be truthful, Darrell and I both know you are mad at us; especially him. We both feel bad about not stopping over here when he got out. And I take full responsibility for being selfish, that's why God is punishing me the most..."

Mary gave Laurell a lopsided look. "And what do you mean by that Laurell?"

Laurell eyes were red from the unshed tears but just as she opened her mouth to speak tears exploded down her cheeks in rivers. "Momma, I'm pregnant. Been throwing up and having bad stomach pains. I took a few test and they are all positive. I saw Darrell today and the police had beat him real bad. He has a few black eyes and a few broken bones…"

Laurell paused. Her emotions had taken over. She closed her eyes imagining her first and only love, pain. *Darrell could be dead. And I'll be stuck out here by myself to raise a child.* She sobbed nonstop until Mary took her into her arms and hugged her tight.

"Momma, they beat him real bad. Then, BC been going around the jail spreading rumors that he's telling on their case, but they don't even have a case. The detective is crooked and tryna turn them on each other." Mary sat quietly rocking Laurell back and forth. She gave her the most endearing motherly console she could give. "Get it out your system baby. I'm listening."

"Not only that but he says he been calling you but you haven't been answering his calls."

Mary released her grip a slight bit just enough to set the record straight. "See what goes around comes around. I love my son to death and I almost died when I found out that he was back in jail. I'm not too pleased to find out about they beating my baby, but I haven't been answering because I want to show him how I felt wen he ignored me. But don't worry about him we need to talk about you and this baby."

Unwelcome tears pricked Laurell's eyes as she clung to Mary. As of now, she was in an emotional turmoil. "Momma, that's the hard part. I'm confused. I don't know what to do. Motherhood is a whole other ball game. Even though we won't admit it, we still act like kids. We still like being in the in-crowd as you use to tell us all the time. And even though they only charging him with a violation, I don't know if we're ready for a child. I mean, I know we don't believe in abortions but I'm confused. I want to keep my baby but I don't know if we are ready.

Marys' mouth went dry for a brief moment. She rumbled through her thoughts and said "Relax and enjoy yourself baby. Motherhood is the best gift life has to offer. Believe me, you going to have a lot more obstacles to get over in life. However, I want you to follow your heart. Your heart won't lead you wrong. And rest assured that whatever decision you decide to make you have a lot of support. Laurell I love you like the daughter I never had."

Mary's heartfelt words brought comfort to Laurell. She smiled and said, "I love you too, Mom."

The two women hugged again and at the love they cherished for one another. "Now, we gotta work together to keep that son of mines out of jail and trouble." Laurell agreed.

$$$

A few hours later, Laurell walked out of Mary's house and got into her Chrysler 300. As soon as she put her seat belt on, her cell phone started to go off. It was a text message from Shady. It read: Damn, sis, you ignoring a nigga? I've been calling you for the past couple days.

Laurell replied:

Bro, you are full of shit. I called you back the other day when I was trying to locate my husband and you didn't answer me.

Laurell sent the message, started the engine, and smashed off. Two minutes later another text came through from Shady. It simply read:

Call me...

Laurell called him. "Hello!" he answered on the first ring.

"What up bro-bro?" Laurell spoke through the phone.

"Shit, where you at sis? And have you heard from your husband?"

Laurell smiled. "Yes. I went to see him today."

"Bout time."

"Boy shut up! Because you know I would have been kicking the doors down for mines if them people wasn't playing games."

"I know that's right homegirl. We all know you one of a kind because most niggaz girls be gone the moment the police put the cuffs on them. I mean, they so scandalous they already thinking who they going to fuck next before the police car even pull off."

Laurell frowned as if Shady could see her "Well not me! I'ma hold my baby daddy down. So yeah nigga, your sis prego."

"What?!" Shady blurted rather unsurprisingly.

"Yep. You might be having a niece or nephew soon. But if anything I want a boy."

"Ha! Truth to the matter all the humping yall was doing right out the gate, I knew it was only a matter of time. However, I think yall gon have a baby girl because you know what they say 'momma's boy, daddy's girl'. I think a little girl would slow Dee Bastard down."

"I agree. I mean, we pray."

"But yeah I do need you to get in contact with ol' boy from the projects and tell him to get in contact with me ASAP. Dee Bastard said you should know who I'm talking about."

"I do."

"Give him my number and tell him to call me."

"Will do."

"Also, tell Kasey fine chocolate ass I said 'hi'."

"Will do. But oh yeah! Did you hear about BC tryna slander my husband's name?"

Shady laughed "Ha! Yeah, I heard about it but it ain't nothing big. Niggas know the real, plus I sent word to BC about the pigs tried to play them, so hopefully he got it."

"But yeah I will call him and get back to you later. I'm driving and don't want to get a ticket."

"Bet that."

Click!

After hanging up Laurell dialed P's number. She explained what she knew to P and gave him Shady's number. She was relieved after hanging up with P. for some unknown reason, she felt like a hundred pounds shackle had been removed from her ankles.

When she made it home, she and Kasey made out for the first time since their threesome with Dee Bastard. That night, she slept like a newborn baby.

Chapter 15

The war was on! The Tiny Mites versus the Tiny Loc Bastardz. BT had set everything up under the watchful eyes of Detective Gilmore. This was a no-win situation for both sides because the corrupt cop on a mad mission believed if he couldn't lock 'em up, let 'em kill themselves. And that's just what he did.

As he watched the Tiny Mites suit up to launch their attack on their big brothers, the TLB's, BT played right-hand man for the puppet master.

"Look yall got to remember what's the first art of war," BT told Lil' Shawn over the phone. Lil' Shawn, Brandon, and Mylo were about to go blast first on the TLB's. "The element of surprise is the first art of war. So make sure yall put it down good."

"That's what we gon do, fa sho."

Lil' Shawn hung up with BT and walked back into his room where his two goons were awaiting their commander and chief. "Look we gon hit them tonight. After this there ain't gon be no more TLB. We gon run the hood, the Tiny Mite. Y'all with me or what?"

"Man, come on, homie, what type of question is that?" ,Brandon, the forever loyal serpent, said.

"Point us in the direction and all of 'em dead," Mylo added.

"Alright cool. We on. Here, everybody grab a burner."

Lil' Shawn emptied a backpack filled with guns on the bed; courtesy of BT. Brandon was the first to retrieve a gun from the litter. He grabbed a Tech-nine. Mylo grabbed a Colt .45. Lil' Shawn tucked two revolvers and a .9mm.

After retrieving their guns, the trio exited the bedroom and walked out to the front door. Detective Gilmore and BT watched as they walked from the porch to the sidewalk, toward the stolen car parked three houses over. As soon as they hopped in the g-ride, Gilmore hit the alert button on his walkie-talkie. Two LAPD squad cars appeared out of nowhere with sirens and red and blue lights flashing.

"Whoooop!"

They pulled up on the car before Brandon could start the engine with the screwdriver in his hand. Lil' Shawn and Mylo hopped out and ran like two track stars going for gold. Brandon, fat and slow, was stuck behind the wheel. "Freeze!" yelled the police in unison with their pistols drawn ready to Swiss cheese the young black thug at any wrong movement. They didn't even bother to go after the runners. Fresh off donut breaks, they settle for the easy catch.

"Man, what fuck is this," BT snapped, looking at Gilmore. "You switched the plan up! Shit wasn't supposed to go down like this. That's bullshit!"

"That's why I'm the cop and you are the snitch. I don't trust you as much as you should trust me. I'm not going to be accessory to murder because you have a vendetta you need to handle. Now, here's the new plan. Fat Boy, right here will be booked on possession of a firearm. Get at your folks and the case will be dropped if I get one of the two: A body or a confession."

BT frowned. "Damn, that's what I get for fuckin' with this cracka," he mumbled.

"Huh? What did you say? Do you have something to tell me? Speak up."

"Nothing, dude! But, so you now want a confession or a body, right? So you want the little nigga to go in there with some wires on?"

"If that will crack the case."

"Man, look… I don't know who you think Dee Bastard and BC is, but if YOU couldn't get them to talk, how could you expect some young puppy to get the job done? You might as well have one of your deputy partners give him a rope and tell him to hang himself. Or give him a knife and tell him to take it to the bank. Matter of fact, I got an idea…"

BT paused, his initial plan had backfired. Now, he had to act fast and think of another plan of action. He couldn't let Gilmore keep putting him in harm's way. From the look of things, the possessed detective was hell bent on getting his fifteen minutes of fame.

"Check this out. I could talk to my boy to have Fat Boy give you a body. Which one you want dead?"

Gilmore smiled. "See now you talking my language. As long as it has nothing to do with me giving you guns and being an accessory I am all for it. You might break under pressure and have me under the bus. Look at you now…"

"Smack! BT smacked his lips like a female. He felt less than a man because not only did he go out the coward way, Gilmore was calling him on it. "Man, the only reason I decided to roll over on my folks is because I'm not with the homies killing homies shit. Plus, you was talking about giving me three strikes for the gun and drugs you found in my house after you and that white bitch set me up."

"Well, BT, I thought at the ripe age of forty you would know the game we, cops, play"

"Anyhow, get out of my car and make me proud."

BT did as he was told. He wasn't used to being treated like shit. Back in his younger days, BT was a wild dude. Everyone respected him. Now, two decades later, he was the top informant in the hood. He put his head down and marched to his car. He had to put together a new plan with Lil' Shawn. He told himself, *After I do this shit I'm skipping town.*

Chapter 16

"Welcome back youngsta. I thought you went home or something," the OG with the sprinkles of gray in his beard said to Dee Bastard as he came walking into the cell. You could tell Dee Bastard had received flashlight therapy as inmates called a brutal beating from police. These beatings were different from getting jumped or beat by inmates. Real convicts could tell the two apart any day.

"Naw, I wish," Dee Bastard replied tossing his bedroll on his bunk. OG was the only occupant in the cell. The other cellmates including the one Dee Bastard had knocked out had been transferred either to Wayside or prison. "The pigs got the best of me."

OG shook his head. "Yeah I see." The old gangsta leapt from his bunk and gave Dee Bastard a hand with his property and getting back situated in the cell. "By the way, my name is OG Ronnie Mack from Hoova. I didn't really get to formally introduce myself last time you was in here, but I see you are a sold lil' brotha."

Dee Bastard stood hunched over with crutches under his arms. He extended his hand to Ronnie. They exchanged Palms. "My name is Dee Bastard from 4 Trey Gangstaz, the TLB clique. But truthfully I'm bout to change my name to TLW which stands for The Leader of the West."

"Why you pushing The Leader of the West? What you rap or something?"

Dee Bastard smiled. "Naw, I write books."

"What kind?"

"Street novels. You know like them hood tales."

"Are you any good youngsta?"

"I wanna believe so." Dee Bastard sat on his bunk and flipped through a folder of papers. "This what I have been working on the week and a half I been in the infirmary."

He handed OG Ronnie the rough draft to a new story he was working on. The first line in the manuscript was something Brother Ajene and Mary use to tell him all the time. It was Proverbs 16:9. "A man's heart plans his way, but the Lord directs his steps."

"WOW! That's deep youngsta. I love that Proverbs. You got me hooked already. But question, do you really believe your heart plans your way, but God directs it?"

"Sure so," Dee Bastard admitted. "I was born in the church. Went faithfully as a kid; but when I got to that age whereas I thought I knew everything I fell deep into the street life."

"I can dig," OG Ronnie said. "We all from the same cloth. I was the same way. So my next question is, where you think God going to direct your steps now?"

"Well, my heart wants me to get out, publish my books, wife my girlfriend, have a family and make my mom's smile. You know, with me in here she has seen a lot of frowns."

"I hear you but I want you to remember Proverbs 11:27 'He who earnestly seeks good finds favor but trouble will come to him who seeks evil."

"Youngsta, I'm telling you all this because I see you got your head on your shoulders and you remind me so much of myself when I was your age. You have a heart of a lion and a brain of a genius. However, you are a troubled young man who needs to find himself. At one point in time, we all have to blossom from boys to men."

Dee Bastard sigh a breath of relief. Even though it seemed like OG Ronnie Mack had turned into Reverend Ronnie Mack in seconds, Dee Bastard knew he needed to hear the wisdom. "Man, I hear you. And talking about Proverbs 12:25 says 'anxiety in the heart of man causes depression, but a good word makes it glad.' And just being able to talk to you about what I need to do when I get out

96

and my dreams and goals make me feel much better. I guess as they say, 'a positive change is a positive plus' right?"

"Youngsta, you ain't never lied. Check this out, God put us back in contact with each other for a reason. He knows my struggles just as he knows yours. I just started writing a Christian novel myself. Check out the prologue and tell me what you think? We could push and help each other."

Ronnie handed Dee Bastard a few pieces of papers that were folded in his Bible. Dee Bastard could tell the original gangsta had been studying the Lord's word from the various notes sticking out of each page. Dee Bastard settled back onto his bunk. He positioned his body upright whereas his collar bone and other wounded body parts wouldn't ache as much. Despite the agony his body was condemned to he sat and read the prologue to Ronnie's manuscript.

It read:

People say that God uses everything and everybody to work out his plan for us. I would learn this to be true after many years of trying to find myself as a troubled man. From gang, drugs, pimping to incarceration, I would eventually learn God has a plan for us all.

For years I was the man on the streets. Well, I thought I was! I had been running the drug supply *on the west side of Los Angeles for many years. I was the leader of one of the largest gangs in America. I had all the beautiful women and all the fancy cars. I was making around $50,000 to $60,000 each week from 1984-1989.*

In 1990, I was incarcerated for a rival gang member murder. I was sentenced to 15 years. Once I got to prison, I started figuring out ways I could continue to make money supplying drugs throughout the prison I was in. I had a big drug network on the streets and had established my name in the drug community amongst pushers and users. I found in jail majority of the people I supplied on the street had found their way in prison with me. It was like prison was the fools' headquarter for congregation and gatherings.

After serious observation and recruitment, I started back supplying drugs. I soon learned that in prison it was harder to distribute the drugs than I had initially thought. I needed a way to get the drugs from one part of the prison to the next. The only way to do that I had to use the church and Lord's name in vein. The church became our transporting route. The only blessing in disguise, I had to become a regular in church and had to sit and listen to every service. Even sing and clap at times.

One Sunday the pastor told me and a few of my friends that we were too old to be in a life of sin such as gangs and drugs. God has a better plan for us. Those words stuck to me like white on rice. A few weeks later, I got down on my knees and asked the Lord forgiveness. By the next year, I had changed my life completely around. But this day I still fight my demons and temptation of fast cars, fast women, fast life, and drugs. My name is Ronnie Mack and here's my testimony...

$$$

"Man, that's a powerful opening, Dee Bastard told Ronnie after reading the prologue. He felt good being in the cell with someone like-minded. *Damn, after I get my ass beat, shit has really been going my way. I only got to knock out a bullet which is only six to twelve months for this violation. Laurell pregnant with my seed. Shady and his so-called attorney who I know he's fucking gone help me start my publishing company. Momma forgave me finally and answered my calls. And now I got a celly who I could relate to. For a nigga to be in jail, I can't be in no better situation. Shit is finally looking up for me. Or is it?*

Dee Bastard slept like a newborn baby that night. Laurell shot him the positive energy they lacked. And all the prayers Mary sent out on her son's behalf was finally paying off.

Chapter 17

Shady and P were shown to their table at Roscoes Chicken and Waffles restaurant in West Los Angeles on Pico Blvd. Shady ordered their number 9 meal which consist of three wings and a waffle. P ordered their Sunshine cocktail and some wings on the side. The very prim waitress smiled broadly and spoke for a few moments with Shady. She had known him from grade school and heard about his mother's death. "How have you been holding up?" she asked.

"I been taking it one day at a time," Shady replied.

"What about your old crew? Like how's Mannie Fresh and what's that Mexican boy name again?"

Shady smiled he remembered all the girls around the school called Dee Bastard, Mannie Fresh. And BC, the Mexican Crip. "Oh, you talking about Darrell and Pedro. They both locked up right now, they'll be out soon. And Darrell writes books so be on the look out for them under NO BRAKES PUBLISHING. His pen name is TLW."

"Oh, that's good. I've never met an author before so as soon as he gets out and publishes his book, tell him to come up here so I could buy one and tell everybody I know him."

"Will do."

"Okay. Yall food will be right with y'all."

The waitress turned on her heels to place their orders. P looked at Shady and said "Man I want to be a TLB so bad. Yall put on for the city. Y'all niggaz known everywhere."

Shady looked P in the eyes. "Little bro, this shit ain't all that it's made out to be. If it was, we wouldn't be here right now. Know what I mean?"

P nodded in agreement. "So what brings us here anyway?" P asked.

"Well, Dee Bastard wanted me to get in contact with you. It's about that work yall put in, you dig?"

P thought back to the night Bo and Smooth were assassinated. He nodded "Yep."

"Here you guys go." The waitress brought over the food and sat it on the table. The two goons immediately filled their face with the best chicken and waffles in California. Roscoe's food is so good even the president, Mr. Obama, and the first lady had stopped by the restaurant a few times.

P and Shady ate in silence until the waitress came back with P's cocktail. Shady enjoyed a glass of water. Though he'd said nothing to indicate it, he wanted a cocktail too. However, after the meeting with P, he planned on meeting up with Zoe Miller.

"So look back to what I was saying before the grub got here…"

"Dee and BC are under the gun right now. The pigs' tryna come up with anything against them. But right now they don't got nothing but this fuck boy named BT…"

P furred his brows. "BT that be at the shop with Big Wrap and 'em?"

"Yea that clown."

"Damn, that old nigga went bad?"

Shady shook his head. "Yea. Niggaz dropping out by the day and will tell on their dying great-grandmom not to do any time."

"I see."

"But yeah the nigga think we don't know he went bad. We gon string him on 'til the right time and feed him to the concrete. My motto is, no body, no murder. Which equals no case. You feel me?"

P nodded, soaking up game and listening at the same time.

"However, where you come in at is yo girl."

P eyes widened. "What about her?"

"Remember she brought a white girl with her to the party that night. I don't know if you know or not but your girl going to know just who we talking about…"

"The bitch name is Charlotte," P confirmed. "I know just who she is."

"Okay. Cool. Look, the fuck boy been fucking with her lately. Make sure you tell your girl, not to tell the white girl nothing about that night. If she already did, somebody gonna have to hush her. Because that boy of hers is the Feds."

"Question: Are we operating on the theory that it's only one person talking or two? Because the white bitch is a whore. She's just like Kioshi, she goes wherever the money is."

"We don't know. Nobody does. You know how these crackaz play. But right now we just got the master of disguise on the hook and that's BT bitch-ass."

P looked around for the waitress. During the brief conversation, he had downed his cocktail. "I need another one of those. I gotta get my mind right hearing all this bullshit."

Shady cracked a one-sided smile. "I can dig it. If I didn't have to handle some business after this I'll be doing the same thing."

"Waitress, can you get another one of these," P said holding up his cocktail. He turned back to Shady. "So I heard they only got a violation, but two more questions: What Dee Bastard say about the case? And did he say anything about me or my boy Sheik names being brought up?"

"No y'all in good standing from what I understand, but he just said the detective is fishing right now. They don't have no case because if they did, someone would already be booked. Nahmean?"

"Yep. So did Dee Bastard say what he's gonna do when he get out because we still got this lick we been having in the making since Central Juvenile Halls. Did he tell you anything about that?"

Shady smiled and shook his head. "Naw he ain't tell me nothing about it. But right now, we on some bigger and better things. We bout to do this book publishing shit, even start a record label or something. You know, switch the game up and watch the money pile up. We bout to be selling books like Muslims sell bean pies. Ha!"

Shady laughed at his own joke but was serious as AIDS in Africa. He was more excited about helping Dee Bastard reach his dreams than the man himself.

"So you trying to be like Slim from Cash Money. You want to be the man behind the scene, but raking in all the dough huh?"

"You damn right. Niggaz gotta be smart nowadays. We can't be in the streets our whole life tryna rob shit, gangbang, and do everything illegal. Shit, look at us now tryna get out of a fucked up situation. The police might be somewhere watching us now."

P agreed "You ain't never lied. I applaud y'all homie but I gotta get it how I live; even if that's robbing the church. Nahmean?"

"Naw I don't know what you mean. You a wild young nigga who I respect but you gotta slow down P. and when you ready me and Dee Bastard will have a job for you in our publishing company. I've heard them vendors and some bookstores don't like paying, so you could be the muscle if you get my drift."

"Well, count me in."

The two young gangsters sat another fifteen minutes at their table conversing before they paid the bill. Shady tipped the waitress a crisp hundred and told her it was nice seeing her. P still high rolling from the heist, did the same. The waitress smiled from ear to ear. She didn't know what Shady did after grade school, but to be giving away crisp hundred dollar bills, she knew he and his boy was on some boss shit. "Alright P. Miller and Puff Daddy, I see y'all doing it big don't forget about me when y'all blow up." She was joking but Shady and P did look like the two wealthy Hip-Hop moguls.

They genuinely smiled at the waitress and headed to their cars. To the blind eyes, these two young black men had the most alluring smiles and humble demeanors, however, beneath the smiles and calm outward appearance, these were two of Los Angeles' deadliest gangsters.

Chapter 18

The sleepy front desk clerk barely even looked up from the book he was reading when he tossed Kioshi a key. The book he was reading was titled 'Girl, I Had Enough'. Kioshi said "Humpft" to herself as she grabbed the key to her room and ushered the almost six feet tall white john to the elevator. The doorman pressed for the fourth floor. The couple rode to the fourth floor. At the room 4328, Kioshi inserted the key. She entered the room ahead of the john. She needed to be one step ahead of the man. She and Charlotte were going to rob this john dry! He was a wealthy grey-haired businessman in his late fifties who was known to keep wads of cash on him.

He closed the door and handed Kioshi ten-hundred. She closed the bathroom door, kicked off her shoes and slid out of her clothes. She stood in her birthday suit. Looking at her light complexion, long wavy hair, long and slender legs, well-shaped ass, and small frame the john started biting on his bottom lip. As he hurried out of his clothes, he thought of how he wanted Kioshi to just urinate on him. A golden shower by a black woman was one of his wildest fantasies. Even though Kioshi looked to be every nationality he could not wait until she showered him with her yellowish body fluids.

107

Riiiiinnng!

Riiiiinnng!

Damn, stop callin', muthafucka!

The ringing stopped and Kioshi grabbed the john by his small three inch penis and forcefully ushered him to the bed. He lay on his back. She was just about to squat over him when the phone rang again.

Riiiiinnng!

Riiiiinnng!

Fuck, if I don't answer the phone and see who it is that muhfucka might call when Charlotte doing her thang and I need this suckaz undivided attention.

"Hold still. Don't move!"

Kioshi retrieved her cell phone and saw that it was P from the caller ID. She answered. "Hello!"

"Where you at?" P asked.

"Working."

"Okay, whatever you doing, don't do it! Stop right now and meet me in the projects."

Kioshi was lost at words. P had never intervened on her getting money even though he hated how she got it. Something in his pitch told her it was best to get out of that room ASAP.

"Hello!" P shot through the other end of the phone. "Did you hear what I just said?! Get your shit and get to the projects now! Oh and don't bring Charlotte with you."

"Okay. I'm on my way."

Kioshi hung up with P, grabbed her clothes, called Charlotte out of the bathroom, and gave the john back his thousand dollars. "Charlotte, this is my friend. My friend this is Charlotte. I gots to go."

Kioshi left them high and dry. She made it from Beverly Hills to Watts, California which is approximately 25 miles away and two cities over, in twenty minutes.

P sat on the hood of his new 745i sipping on a fifth of Hennessy. He had on a pair of shell toe Adidas with matching sweatpants and sweatshirt. In the hood, better yet, the projects, you could tell when a person was up or down. And P was up! Being a stick-up kid, everyone around the maze structured projects knew he was fresh off a lick, as people in the streets called a heist or come up.

"What's so important or urgent that you just made me miss out on a few G's?" Kioshi said hopping out of her black on black 2004 Kia Sportage.

"I believe your freedom is better than a few racks, right?" P said passing her the bottle of fiery liquor.

Kioshi took the bottle and turned it up like a pro. She leaned on the hood of P's 745i and replied. "What you know that I don't?"

"A lot," P answered. "But look yo' girl been fucking with that nigga BT right?"

"Yep. But she says his big black ass pay what he weighs."

"Alright cool but that nigga working with the police about that shit with the nigga who spit on you and that shootout at the party."

"How you know he's telling?"

"Because I know!" P snapped. "Just know that the bitch-boy is no good. However, the thing is he don't know we know. So I need you not to tell Charlotte. If anything try talking her into not messing with the nigga."

"You already too late. She told me that she stopped fucking with him because not only was he talking about love but the police had kicked in his door last time she was there talking about guns and drugs. I don't know, but I'm not going to say nothing to her about him."

"Why you didn't tell me about him getting raided. I swear I'm starting to get real bad vibes about Charlotte, you might need to cut that bitch loose."

Kioshi passed P back the fifth after she took a few swallows of the liquor. She screwed her face at the burning sensation moving down her throat. "Man, Charlotte the homegirl. She's cool peoples. She's about getting her money. And I think you really don't like her because she's white and she's a whore just like me. You don't like what I do so you look at her as a bad influence."

"That might be it but you know what they say; when you get bad vibes about a person it's usually something shady about them."

"I agree but we both know why you don't like her or got bad vibes about her."

P turned the bottle up and grabbed Kioshi by the booty. "I'd rather be safe than sorry. But on a real note, I want you to promise me you going to watch what you say around her at least 'til we figure out what's going on."

"I promise."

"That's what I'm talking about. You know I got your best interest at heart and love you right? P stood in front of Kioshi as she leaned on the car. He held her by the waist and passionately kissed her on the lips. Their love was a "ghetto love" story waiting to be told.

Kioshi kissed him back with the same passion. "Yes I know you love meand got my best interest at heart. That's why I come running when you call. Percy, I tell you all the time I love you."

He kissed her again. This time a French kiss. "Kioshi, have you been keeping your eyes and ears to the streets for me?"

"Don't I always?" She kissed him back. "And you getting me wet and horny on the hood of your car."

In the Nickerson Garden Projects where they grew up, it would not have been anything out of the ordinary if they would have got it on right then and there. However, P had other things on his mind. "We could put the flame out later."

"Right now, I need to know what you been hearing and I need you to ride with me to check on this lick me and Dee Bastard been working on for some years now."

Kioshi grabbed P by the crotch. "That's why I love you because you think 'MOB', money over bitches. Any other nigga will be tryna hit this sweet pussy right here. I love you, Percy."

"I love you too. But answer my question." P demanded.

"Well, over towards the 4 Trey's they say some nigga named Lil' Shawn is like the man now. Pooh and Keisha fuck with two of his boys. You know how your sister and Pooh rat-ass get around. I think the niggaz names that they fuck with is Brandon and Mylo. Keisha fucks with Brandon and they say he just got locked up the other day for a gun. They got a clique in the 4 Trey's called Tiny Mites. They supposed to be the little homies of the TLB's but from what Pooh told me, Mylo told her that they bout to take over. I don't know what that supposed to mean but you know how them niggaz down there all want to be the man and kill each other all the time over power."

P shook his head. "You ain't never lied. The 4 Trey's are one gang I could say is really divided by cliques. Them niggaz define the saying 'too many chiefs and not enough Indians'. But yeah good looking on the update. If you hear anything else let me know. Now, let's go do our homework on this lick."

P forever on a come up was going to rob Calvin, his old cellmate from juvenile detention, and his father with or without Dee Bastard. He was a true stick-up kid and Calvin and his father had what he wanted: money!

'After I get done studying these niggaz, I'ma Call Shady and give him the heads up about what I just heard about them Tiny Mites niggaz'.

P shook his head as he and Kioshi hopped in her car headed toward Calvin's residence. "Man, niggaz gon' learn the hard way about just pillow talking to bitches they barely know."

Chapter 19

"I'm telling y'all, everybody knows Bastard Child. BC! I'ma muhfuckin loc! Niggaz know about the Mexican Crip. On Tiny Loc Bastardz I'm one of the niggaz who started this gangsta shit..."

BC was in a six-man cell with four other inmates whom all happen to be Crips from other sub-chapters of the Crip organization. You had TD from Main Street Crip, Cas Boo from 89 East Coast Crip, Tone Bone from Under Ground Crip, and Lil' CoCo from 87 Gangsta Crip. The Quartet of Crips plus BC were all young reputable Crips within their sub-chapters. Throughout the day they had all traded war stories back and forth. To this group of rowdy Crips this was their favorite pastime. Their life all consisted of, sex, money, murder, Crippin', and mayhem.

BC had the floor and he was letting it be known that he was the Crip of all Crips. He didn't care who was around him because couldn't no one step to the almighty Bastard Child.

"Aww, Cuzz, sit down with all that high power shit," TD said. "Nigga, you is a Mexican. Lucky we let you walk the mainline as much as we beefing with the Mexicans around here."

"Yeah," Tone Bone stood. He was around six feet tall and cut up. He was big like the actor Terry Crew from the movie "Friday After Next" and "White Chicks."

"Hol' on," Cas Boo jumped from his bunk. "Y'all can't tag team the homie. Y'all know how the 4 Trey's and East Coast's do."

"On Movin," Lil' CoCo leapt from his bunk. "What y'all two niggaz talking about because I'm riding with BC. Y'all know how the Eastside Gangstaz move.

It was a three against two standoff. This was another thing the young Crips did to pass time. They fought, wrestled, and horse-played day in and day out. To them, jail was just part of the territory and lifestyle they lived and only the strong survived. Before anyone could blink an eye, Tone Bone had rushed Cas Boo and Lil CoCo and BC took TD. The tribe of young rowdy Crips flung each other from one side of the cell to the next. It was a royal rumble.

Biiiiinnng!

Cliiing!

Cling!

Silence. The cell grew still and quiet like a church when the pastor tells everyone to bow their heads. Someone out of the bunch had dropped their shank. In jail, everyone knew the sound of solid metal hitting the ground. "Oh shit my bad," BC said breaking the silence. "I dropped my burner."

He had a sinister grin on his face but knew he had messed up.

"Aww nigga," Lil CoCo said looking at BC. "Cuzz, I was riding with you and you drop the burner during a rumble. What if this was a real melee, you would have fumbled."

Cas Boo chimed in. "Aww cuzz on East Coast Crip you gotta get disciplined for that..."

Bing! Bing!

Before Cas Boo could finish talking BC took off on him. He knew he had to get chastised for a deadly mistake. Even though the tribe of young Crips took the horse-play as a pass time, it was also a form of training for war. Just like in the military, in jail, there was no telling when a war or riot was going to kick off.

The two piece left-right combination caught Cas Boo off guard and landed on the forehead and jaw. Cas Boo light complexion and tattooed face lit up beet red and he instantly responded with an uppercut. The rest of the Crips sat back and

watched; then Lil' CoCo jumped in helping Cas
Boo. The discipline lasted a brief 43 seconds since
BC was from 4 Trey. Tone Bone and TD kept a
record of this and broke up the fight once the time
was up. "Alright. Alright," they said in unison
jumping between BC and the two attackers.

BC had a busted lip and nose. Cas Boo had a
knot the size of a golf ball on his forehead. Lil'
CoCo did not have one battle mark on him. BC
wasn't feeling that. He felt blood for blood was a
fair exchange. He rushed Lil' CoCo with the same
two piece combination he had served Cas Boo with.
The left punch caught CoCo in the jaw. CoCo
ducked the right one and Bastard Child punch
landed fist first to the iron bars. Boom! Crack!

From the sound of impact and the pain that
instantly shot through his body, BC knew he had
broken a bone or two in his hand. "Aarg Cuzz!" he
whined. "I just fucked up."

The cell went still again. All eyes were on BC.
Everyone knew he had damaged his hand, by the
way, he was holding it. He had ran straight to his
bunk and rolled on it from side to side in agony.
"Aww cuzz, I think I broke my shit." He was in
pain. A lot of pain!

"You want us to call man down," TD asked.

"Hell naw, I'm bout to gangsta this shit out,"
BC replied.

In jail, going man down was looked upon in a bad way. Most inmates took it as a weakness. BC had a reputation to uphold. He was the notorious Bastard Child from the dangerous TLB clique.

"Aye youngstaz yall alright up there?

"Aiyo, cell number 3! Yall cool in there?"

Other inmates on the tier heard all the commotion and knew they had to check on the young rowdy Crips here and there because they were known to be beating each other up and bringing harm to the weakest link in the cell. That was the reason their last cellmate that they called sixth man rolled it up out of the cell by running to the deputy.

After an hour passed and things had settled down, BC still lay in agony. His had had swollen to the size of a cantaloupe. He needed medical attention but refused to go "man down". He decided to wait until the morning and go to sick call when the deputies opened the cells. He decided to hop on the phone since Cas Boo, the phone bandit and pretty boy of the cell, wasn't on it.

He called Laurie.

"This is Global Tel Link, you have a collect call from…"

"BC!"

"To accept this call press one…"

"Thank you for using Global Tel Link."

"Hello!"

"What up mommy," BC said into the phone hearing his junior high sweetheart on the other end of the phone.

"Shit nothing, been waiting on you to call me. What took you so long?"

"Aww shit! My dumb ass was in here fucking around with my weird-ass cellies and probably broke my hand."

"Did you go get it checked out? Laurie asked concerned.

"Naw you know up in here a nigga gotta Crip it out. Nahmean?"

"I hear you but I'm not saying I agree. But I talked to Shady today and he said to tell you to kick back on letting the pigs get the best of y'all. He said that man trying to divide and conquer. He even beat Dee Bastard so bad he just getting out of the infirmary. Shady said y'all are like brothers so calm down with the bullshit. He gave me $200 to put on your books. He also said do yo' little violation and come home…"

"FISH ON THE LINE"

As BC talked on the phone the module deputy yelled: "FISH ON THE LINE" through the PA system. This meant new inmates had arrived.

Bastard ignored the warning. He kept to his business on the phone. But the other Crips in the cell stood at attention awaiting the new arrivals. This was the moment of truth. This was the moment anything could happen. A friend or foe could have easily walked into the cell and these Crips were sharks in the ocean of fish.

Before the fish could even step half way into the cell, Tone Bone was on him. "Where you from cuzz?"

"I'm from Eastside 4 Trey Gangstaz,"the new arrival said. "I'm from the Tiny Mite clique."

All eyes turned toward BC in the back of the cell on the phone. Unspoken words from the other Crips to BC was *do you know him?* If BC would have given an uncertain look or glare as if saying he didn't know the fish, the sharks would have attacked. But BC knew the fat chubby kid. He knew him well. He watched the kid grow up.

"Baby I'ma call you back alright?"

"SMACK! Laurie smacked her lips. "how you just going to hang me up and waste my minutes to talk to them niggaz in jail?"

"Little Brandon just walked in my cell. Let me holler at him right quick."

"Lashonda's fat-ass brother?"

"Yes," BC said with a half laugh.

"What that nigga doing in jail?"

"I don't know. But bout to find out."

"Okay. I love you. But be careful around that nigga. How shit going around the hood no telling what he really in jail for."

BC cracked a one-sided smile. "Ma you ain't never lied. And I love you too tell Shady he's right and good looking on that change and I love him and my nigga Dee Bastard. We all we got."

"Okay. Will do. But just remember what I said about Brandon," Laurie said. Something just wasn't sitting right with her that Brandon was in the cell with BC. It probably was because BC had cheated on her with Brandon's sister Lashonda, but who Lashonda haven't slept with? However, it was something about the situation Laurie was not feeling.

BC agreed and hung up. "Brandon what up fat cuzz," he said greeting the younger 4 Trey.

"Aww BC what cuzz," Brandon said smiling from ear to ear.

The two 4 Trey gang members greeted each other with a dap and a brotherly hug. BC protected his right hand the whole time. "Damn, cuzz what happened with yo' hand?"

"I just fucked it up Crip. What up with you doe? What they got you in here for?"

Brandon shook his head as he walked his bedroll on the empty bed bunk.

"Man, they got me for a burner." He parted the other Crips like the Red Sea. The sharks all moved to at-ease position. BC had certified this fish. He was gangsta approved. BC introduced him to all the sharks in the tank and they all greeted the young goon with daps and "what up cuzz!"

An hour or so later, BC was back on the floor with the spotlight on him. One thing about BC, he loved attention and hated feeling like he was not the man. He was known to have Tupac Syndrome and when it kicked in, BC was a real live character.

"Brandon, tell these niggaz how the Mexican Crip get down out there."

Brandon vouched for BC and what he was telling the other Crips.

"Tell these niggaz how the TLB's run the whole hood and I'm one of the niggaz who started Tiny Loc Bastardz."

Once again, Brandon vouched for BC but in the back of his head he could not help but think about why he was in jail and how Lil' Shawn stated that the TLB's felt they run the hood and planned on taking out the Tiny Mites. BC had just verified that Lil' Shawn was right. The TLB's did have a hit on them. Inside his bedroll was a ten-inch homemade knife that the deputy put there. When he handed the bedroll to Brandon he said "This from Lil' Shawn." Upon seeing what was inside before making it to the cell, he told himself "Lil' Shawn did say he's connected all over the world due to the fact his brother was the notorious Bastard Don". However, little did Brandon know it was not Lil' Shawn behind the conspiracy, it was the puppet master, Detective Gilmore.

"Cuzz, furthermore tell these niggaz who really started Tiny Mites and how that came about?"

"The Tiny Mites is a clique me and my niggaz Lil' Shawn and Mylo started. The name come from the homie brother Dynasty because he used to call us Tiny Mites and we were his little homies and we looked up to the TLB's."

Bastard Child shook his head. That wasn't the answer he was seeking. The attention possessed TLB became irritated. He was the notorious Bastard Child. If one wasn't with him one was against him. Despite the grueling pain from his broken hand, BC snapped. "Cuzz, alright fuck it. Since you don't want to tell them the truth about how the Tiny Mites started, tell these niggaz how yo' sister Lashonda started being a hoodrat and your sister Rose be stalking my crime partner and how she'll drop anything to suck his dick whenever he call because she say she his best friend but really want to take Laurell place…"

BC went on attack mode. It was true that he was one of the first homeboys to turn Lashonda out before she became community pussy. However, what he said about Dee Bastard and Rose, half of it was true, the other half lies. Brandon stood next to his bunk heated. BC kept going paying Brandon no attention. The other Crips laughed and instigated as BC roasted his younger homie.

"And yeah, I ain't even saying, nigga, how I used to be having my dick over your head while I was fucking your sister in the butt and you on the room floor sleep. Did…"

"You bitch-ass nigga laugh about this…"

Brandon pulled out his shank and stabbed BC in the chest. BC jumped back and touched over his heart where he'd just been stabbed. In a state of shock, he frowned and reached for his knife at waist level, but about this time Brandon had caught everyone by surprise and plunged in and out of BC over five times hitting major arteries.

"Aww cuzz did this bitch-ass nigga just stabbed me?" BC said out loud more out of shock than to anyone specifically. He rumbled while trying to retrieve his knife. With his fight hand being wounded he had to fight off Brandon and get his weapon with his left hand. About time he got a firm grip on his knife, he had been stabbed over fifteen times. Through rage and fear of defeat he managed to stab Brandon twice, once in the eye and the other in the stomach. Brandon attack came to an abrupt end once he lost sight in his left eye. He stepped back from BC and the Mexican Crip could have finished the young gangsta off, but BC's body went still. The blood in his heart had stopped pumping. The dark cloud of death filled the cell. BC lifeless body fell to the floor headfirst even cracking his skull on impact.

Silence filled the tier and every module throughout the jail. It was something about death that made the world go still. It could have been the smell, the silence, or the bloodshed. Whatever it was the place grew still and quiet. One would say from the legacy the notorious Bastard Child, the Mexican Crip would leave behind. Even the concrete walls within the cell wept the loss of a great Crip soldier. Even worst that night Dee Bastard felt it. He tossed and turned in his sleep. He woke up with tears in his eyes. His heart was beating at half pace. His head was spinning like he

126

had been clubbed. He vomited all over himself. He figured it was either from the reoccurring nightmares he had of Detective Gilmore coming back to get him or the fact that he was suffering the side effect of having a woman pregnant. However, he would, later on, find out these emotions were from the cell and the coroner's removal of BC's body. Brandon was taken to the hole and charged with BC's murder. As he sat in the hole he paced his cell back and forth. He was losing his mind from the guilt of killing a man, but the evil side of darkness turned him into a beast. He held the bars and rattled the cage until the tier grew quiet. He then yelled "TINY MITES OR NOTHING!"

A monster had been born.

Chapter 20

The funeral procession rode into Los Angeles County Memorial Cemetery off of Manchester and La Brea in Inglewood, California next to the Great Western Forum. The body of Pedro Guzman aka Bastard Child was being put to rest. Crips pulled into the maze structure cemetery by the thousands. Crips came from all over to pay their respect to the Mexican Crip. T-shirts with BC's face were printed and passed out. This home going was packed, to say the least.

BC was carried by TLB pallbearers to the unmarked grave. The preacher Rev. JM Daily preached about the afterlife and how the lord cleansed the sins and guilt that the world had done to the innocent soul that was being put to rest. He said, "Psalms 107 says…"

"They sat in darkness and in the shadow of death, bound in affliction and irons and there was no one to help. They cried out to the lord in their trouble and he saved them from their distress. He brought them out of the darkness and broke their chains into pieces."

"Job 17: 11, 15…"

"My days are past, my purposes are broken off, and even the thoughts of my heart, where then are my hope?"

"Lord, today as you accept Pedro Guzman in those pearly white gates of Heaven and free him of pain, all his dark days, we ask that you bless his family, friends, and loved ones..."

"All has arisen; all has fallen, ashes to ashes, dust to dust..."

Mrs. Maria Guzman sobbed helplessly at the sight of the casket bearing her son's body being lowered into the grave. Momma Mary stood beside her patting her on the back. Tears streamed down her face too. BC was also Mary's son. As the two mothers watch the casket fall below ground level, their emotions flared high and screams of "why Lord!" filled the air.

"Why?!" Mrs. Guzman fell to Her knees. The pain she felt was unexplainable. She was not supposed to outlive her son. He was just an innocent baby in her eyes. "Why?! Pedro, why?!"

Only a mother who had lost a child knew her pain. She hardly noticed the tall, well-dressed man step to her and lifts her from the ground. The young man looked familiar but it was hard seeing through her watery eyes. He placed his arm around her tenderly and ushered her to the family limo awaiting her.

"Come on, Mrs. Guzman, I'll take you to the limo. I'm very sorry about what happened," the man said. "I took care of everything. Here's the money for the funeral."

The man pressed an envelope filled with cash into the distraught mother's hand. Mrs. Guzman threw the envelope to the ground. "I don't want no money. I want my son!" Even though she was of Spanish descent, Mrs. Guzman acted just as her son did, black.

"Maria, that's Andre," Mary informed, "That's Pedro and Darrell friend. The one we like."

Mrs. Guzman opened her eyes and zoned in on the man. Through her sunglasses and watery eyes, she knew Shady's smile and peanut head. "Shady, baby, I apologize." Mrs. Guzman knew out of all people Shady knew her pain. It seemed like yesterday, she and Mary were consoling him as he watched his mother be put to rest,

"I understand," Shady said picking up the envelope filled with fifty and hundred dollar bills. "I understand." He held her tight.

On the other side of the funeral, Lil Shawn watched Shady talking to BC mother. He followed their every move. He was sizing Shady up. To him, one reputable TLB was down and he and the Tiny Mites had two more to go. "Mylo, you put the tracking device on that bitch nigga car?" he asked.

130

"Yep," Mylo answered.

However, as Lil Shawn followed Shady's every move, P watched his every move. The hunter was being hunted for lack of definition. In addition to that, P had Kioshi and Sheik spread out. Kioshi job was to get up under the young goon and fuck the life out of him. A skilled prostitute and the most venomous snake in the garden, this mission was a piece of cake. Sheik was there just in case something was to crack off.

As Kioshi made her way toward Lil Shawn, P looked over to Seven and his crew. Seven was the undisputed leader of the 97 East Coast Crip clique called NHT (Niggaz Havin' Thangz). He was Dee Bastard's younger cousin by Mary's sister Sam. Sam had once dated Big Wrap so Seven was no doubt trained and learned from the best. P didn't know Seven that good but just as Seven had heard of him, P had heard of Seven. The two young generals nodded at each other. From the beginning of the TLB era in Los Angeles, a secret tribunal watched over them guiding their progress through key street players from the city. Dee Bastard called them "the guardians" "the Black Knight", two young men whose decisions were absolute and often brutal.

No one knew Seven and P were the Black Knights. Two kids Dee Bastard felt worthy to trust with his own life because he trained them at a

131

young age how to act and think like him. Even though the official TLB were now considered endangered species and the original reputable member on the streets was Shady, the Black Knights were there as re-enforcement.

After the two known generals acknowledged each other, P went back to hunting the hunter. He followed Lil Shawn at a close yet sizable distance just in case the young goon tried to pull something slick on Kioshi. Nothing popped off and Lil Shawn bit the bait.

"I'ma call you tonight, Sexy," Lil Shawn said smiling like the cat who stole the canary. He just knew with him being the man in power dime pieces like Kioshi were at his disposal or were they? As always the position of power was a blessing and a curse. What was it going to be for Lil Shawn?

Kioshi countered "Naw, I'm going to call you, Little Daddy."

Still cheesing, Lil Shawn said, "Yea do that beautiful."

After Kioshi walked back over toward P, she smiled inwardly. P knew she would forever be his Bonnie, and he would forever be her Clyde. Their ghetto love was one in a million. However, as P thought about him and Kioshi something stood out about Lil Shawn. It was the gold chain around his neck with a medallion that could have been well worth over $25,000. It read: "TINY MITES or NOTHING" in brick format. A stick-up kid at heart, P laughed to himself.

Chapter 21

The first person Big Wrap saw when he entered, 'Due 2 The Fact' pool hall off of 41st Street and San Pedro was BT. BC's repast was being held here. Pictures of BC were lined all around the place. There were so many Crips in there, Big Wrap wasn't sure if it was a repast or Rec on Cell Block C (the Crip module) in the county jail. From first sight, he was impressed. "Yes, they sending the little homie out in style. Whoever decorated this place did the damn thang."

Big Wrap became frozen in time upon seeing BT. After the meeting, he had with Shady at Friday's he had seen the change in BT's swag, behavior and everything. The guilt was eating away at him and Wrap could tell it was even haunting him while he slept. BT was losing weight and smoking cigarettes like a chimney. On the outside, he played it cool, but his conscious was eating away at him from the inside.

Big Wrap walked over to the snitch and his eye turned swollen red from the unshed watery tears. He wanted dearly to just punch BT in the mouth then pistol-whip him over the head before flat lining him. Not only that, but BT sensed Big wrap was on to his betrayal because he was literally shaking like a snitch at a gangsta party.

Big Wrap played it cool, calm, and collected . He knew BT was on borrowed time, just as he knew his date of birth. There was no doubt in his mind that his ex-partner in crime and running mate was the bad apple. He patted BT on the back. "What's good, BT?"

BT could not look Big Wrap in the eyes. He forced a smile that Big Wrap knew was counterfeit. "Aww shit man just paying my respects to the little homie."

Bullshit! Big Wrap thought. *Nigga, you came to retrieve information for them, white folks. Nigga, we on to you and your shenanigans.*

"I hear you. But why you ain't been fucking with your boy lately? Nigga, you use to be at the shop with me every day. It's like you been distancing yourself from us. You alright?"

BT tilted his head to the ground. He couldn't hide the guilt on his conscience if his life depended on it. And it did! *This nigga dead as a door knob,* Big Wrap thought.

"Naw, Wrap I been down with the flu. This cold been wearing a nigga out."

"Well, you gotta stay healthy. Nahmean?"

"Sure do. But yeah what's been up with you? What's been going on? What's the word? What they been talking about around here with the BC shit?"

A few weeks ago, Big Wrap would have thought nothing of BT questions; however, a five fire alarm went off in his head. *Man, no this weirdo didn't just insult my intelligence. Let me get out this dude's face before I knock his ass out and blow my disguise that I know he's a snitch.*

"Aww, shit man you ain't missing nothing out here. Stay where you at and get over that flu, But shit I gotta get in traffic and go grab some appliances for the shop. I'll get at you later."

Big Wrap turned on his heels before BT could respond. Big Wrap did not want to give off the vibe that he suspected any foul play, but he could not muster the thought of conversing with the snitch nor shaking his hand. The good thing as soon as Big wrap turned around Shady was walking into the pool hall. Big Wrap played it off. "Shady!" he called walking toward the young gangsta.

Shady's eyes lit up seeing Big Wrap and BT. Big Wrap hurried over. "What's good old man?" Shady said as Big Wrap made it over to him. "I see the snitch done made it to the gangsta party."

Big Wrap slapped Shady five and they shared a brotherly hug. He whispered in Shady's ear "Yeah that nigga telling fasho. We gotta kill the cancer

136

before it keeps spreading. But I'm outta here before I do it in front of the whole hood."

"Naw don't do that," Shady replied "As you see, we are the minority. Eighty percent of these niggas in here are ready to drop a dime on me and you. Snitching is at an all time high. And you know most of these cats want real niggas like me and you out the way. I mean, look at the lil nigga Lil Shawn, over there gossiping with the snitch like it's the thing to do."

Big Wrap looked over his shoulders and just that fast, BT and Lil Shawn was indulged in what looked to be a deep conversation. "Damn!" Big Wrap blurted. "The sad part we can't even lace the young nigga with the game because we really don't know where he stands."

Shady shook his head in agreement "Like Jay-Z says in that song : It's a secret society all we ask is trust."

"Ha! You ain't never lied youngsta. But this life we live sho ain't no secret society because we can't trust none of these suckas."

Big Wrap shook his head at the thought of his own words. 'If a nigga hangs around nothing but suckas what does that make me?'

"Shady, just thinking about it, we are the crowd we keep."

Shady looked Big wrap in the eyes. "I have been feeling like that since my moms died. I could truly say shit ain't been the same since my queen left me but all this shit just been opening my eyes. I'm done after this homie. I was just telling Zoe in the car..."

Big Wrap eyes widened. He cut Shady off. "You got that fire lawyer chick in the hood at some shit like this?"

Shady smiled knowing where Big Wrap was headed with the conversation. "Before you chew me out let me tell you, she wanted to ride to the burial with me. The only reason I bought her here was because Momma Mary told me to make sure I come get me and her a plate and BC's mom flipped out on me when I put the money in her hands for the funeral so I'm bout to pay for everything and get on."

"So where's Zoe?"

"She's outside in the car. She acted like she really wanted to see how I use to live and be supportive of me while I mourn the loss of another loved one, but as soon as I pulled up here, she saw all these Crips and got scared."

Big Wrap furred his brow. "Nigga, I'd be scared too. Shit, nigga, I'm scared now! And I'm a reputable Crip. Man, get that woman out of the hood!"

Shady sensed the urgency in Big Wrap's voice. He shook his mentor hand one last time. Wrap looked his protegee in the eyes. "Let me ask you again… Are you fucking her yet? Because she's digging you. Remember I told you that at Friday's, she is."

Shady facial expression gave Big Wrap the answer he needed before he could respond. For the first time in his life, Shady was in love. He smiled "Yes Big Homie! Between me and you, that's my misses. We have been dating for a minute now, but as you would say the right hand never let the left know what he's doing."

"I could dig it, but make sure you hurry up and get her out of here because I'm gone. I can't stand being around this crowd any longer."

Big Wrap looked over his shoulders again. This time Lil Shawn had disappeared, but BT was talking to another person.

"As you see the agent at work and we ain't tryna be on nobody's case, in no pictures, or no recordings. Hit me when you and beautiful make it to where yall going."

The original gangsta and young gangsta exchanged daps and parted ways.

Chapter 22

Riiiiinnnnng!

Riiiiinnnnng!

"Fuck, it's dark as fuck out here. Cuzz, we done followed this nigga all the way to the back woods of Ku Klux Klan land. Nigga, I don't even know where the fuck we at. And plus that beautiful red bone bitch from earlier keep calling a nigga. Mylo, I'm telling you nigga, the Tiny Mites are on! Nigga, we on!"

Mylo shook his head from the passenger seat, the pair of Tiny Mites followed Shady and Zoe Miller to the desert. "Yeah, nigga the hood is really ours. Brandon got that bitch-ass nigga BC. We bout to get Shady bitch-ass now. And Dee Bastard we'll worry about him when we cross that bridge."

The two Tiny Mites kept their eyes on Shady's vehicle. They shared laughter and potent blunts of Kush as they followed their prey. The chase had begun and the pair was anticipating death like two wolves chasing a rabbit.

"Cuzz, we bout to kill this nigga and rob him at the same time," Lil Shawn told Mylo. "You saw the money he had on him at the funeral when he tried to give it to BC momma."

One car ahead, Shady spotted the white Honda Accord following him. He looked at Zoe and said "Baby, I'm not hundred percent sure but I think someone is following us, so keep your head straight forward, don't panic, and do whatever I tell you to do."

Zoe Miller's eyes widened. She did exactly as told but she knew the life Shady led. Even though around her he presented himself as a gentleman and a scholar she knew his childhood wasn't so colorful. For lack of definition, he was a street guy, no telling who could have been following them. Her heart started pumping rapidly. She tried to hide the fear she felt inside, but for a woman who had lived a very peaceful life and raised by a family filled with prestigious lawyers, doctors, and politicians; beads of sweat formed on her forehead. She began to panic.

"Andre, what do you mean someone is following us?" She kept her head straight forward but wanted badly to turn and see who Shady was talking about. "Just pull over."

"Pull over!" Shady repeated. "Zoe, are you that naïve? This is life or death. That's not the police behind us. If so, I'll pull over when they flash the lights and sirens."

Shady turned onto a dark street three blocks away from Zoe's house. The white Honda Accord did the same thing. He drove another two blocks and made a right. The white car did the same thing. 'Turn left. Turn right. Left. Right. Right. Left.' He thought and drove block after block. The white car followed his every move. Whoever was behind him wasn't that smart nor that good at disguising themselves.

Lil Shawn and Mylo was following Shady's every move like they had planned. But the two goons' brains were only as big as peanuts. Shady could have been driving them into a death trap and they would have driven right into it.

"Cuzz, this nigga must be lost or he stays deep into the boon docks," Mylo said. "I'm getting tired of following this nigga. Let's just catch him in the hood…"

Riiiiinnnng!

Riiiiinnnng!

Mylo cell phone began to ring. He looked at the screen. It read: Pooh. He looked at Lil Shawn and smiled. "Hol' on let me see what my project bitch want." He answered. "Hello!"

"What you doing, Daddy?" Pooh asked in her most seductive voice. Mylo didn't know the woman he thought was his secret lover was really a set-up artist. Once P had informed Kioshi to keep her ears to the streets within the 4 Trey territories, she

142

recruited her two partners in crime, Keisha, and Pooh. It did not take long for the two hood girls to make their way into the demise of the Tiny Mites.

"I'm in traffic. Why you miss a young nigga already? That dick good huh?" Mylo asked grabbing his crotch and showing off in front of his boy. He put Pooh on speaker.

"Come on , Daddy, you know I love you because I'm right here right now with my homegirl. She said she met one of your homeboys today at a funeral and he's fine as hell."

"Yea the 4 Trey's are known to be some cool niggas, especially the Tiny Mites. But what she say the homie name is?"

Lil Shawn started smiling inwardly. He tapped Mylo on the arm and whispered. "I bet that's the red bone bitch I cracked earlier she talking about. Who else from the hood who's flier than me?"

"She said his name is Lil Shawn. Do you know him?" Pooh already knew the answer, but she knew Kioshi and her had to play these teenyboppers to win the game. And they were no match for these vixens.

"Yeah I know Lil Shawn. We together right now. Matter of fact, put yo' girl on the phone."

Pooh put Kioshi on the phone and Mylo handed his phone to Lil Shawn. He spoke into the speaker. "What up sexy?"

Kioshi put on her most enticing voice. "You the sexy one. You fine with yo' young ass. I could just see yo' young ass fucking the shit out of me. Ha! Naw, let me stop playing with you because we both know you are not ready for no real redbone in your life."

Lil Shawn was all smiles. He was smiling so much, he was at a loss for words. Damn, this bitch is with the business he thought. Kioshi's bluntness caught this rookie off guard and all he could do was smile from ear to ear.

"Hello! Do the cat got your tongue? Oh, my bad! The cat ain't got your tongue or none of that dick yet but are you there I mean?"

Mylo started giggling on the passenger side of the seat. Lil Shawn the forever egotistic frowned "Bitch, you got me fucked up. I'm Lil Shawn. I'ma fuck the shit out yo' big booty ass and stick this big dick in your mouth."

"Psst." Kioshi shot through the phone. "So when that going to happen because me and Pooh got a room right now, and I been calling you for the past couple hours and you been acting like you scared of a bitch or something."

"Ha!" Lil Shawn shouted into the phone. "Bitch, once again, I'm Lil Shawn the mutha fuckin' man on these streets. Bitch ain't never scared. We'll hit y'all up when we get done handling our business."

Click. Lil Shawn hung up and tossed Mylo back his phone. "Okay. Let's pull up on this nigga and serve him. We got some pussy lined up. And like they said ain't no pussy better than new pussy"

Up ahead Shady was trying to calm Zoe Miller down. With panicking and whoever following them speeding up, his better judgment became clouded. *Damn, what do I do*, he thought. *I don't want to scare Zoe any more than she already is. I shouldn't have even told her we were being followed. Damn, these niggas whoever they are is speeding up. I gotta get my burner out the stash, but Zoe going to really panic. But nigga so what, you gotta protect y'all. Plus, damn, it ain't just us I'm protecting. She just told me earlier that she's pregnant. I gotta do something!*

As Shady thought Lil Shawn was gaining on him. He turned down a well-lit street. In the rearview mirror, he spotted a gold chain glistening from the driver's neck. He thought back to the funeral and repast. In the flick of a thumb, he knew who was following him, Lil Shawn!

"Okay. Baby, listen real good to me. I know who's behind me. It's some young dude who's trying to make a name for himself. So, look, I got to get you out of this car. What I'ma do is pull to the back of the house so you run through the neighbor's backyard and sneak around the front of your house. I'ma keep going…"

"Wait. Wait!" Zoe cut Shady off. "Andre I am not leaving your side. I have a better idea, just go pull up to the Sheriff's station. I could call them."

Lil Shawn and Mylo was now on their bumper lurking like a thief in the night. "Zoe, please, just take my word. We don't have any time. Now, as soon as I bend this corner, run through the neighbor yard to the back of your house and go inside until I make it in."

As Shady instructed Zoe he retrieved his Beretta .9mm from the stash. *I ain't never use this burner but I got seventeen shots for these suckas. But the best thing to do is get Zoe out of the car, get back on the freeway, and punch it back to the hood, and have a [W…] on deck. Matter of fact, I could call P and Sheik. Them two niggas stay ready to kill shit.*

Shady thought of every possibility. His life was on the line and he was trying to escape death the best way he could, but when the man up above calls your number, it's time to leave earthly things behind.

When they reached the spot for Zoe to jump out and run, she fumbled with the door handle which cost them valuable seconds and Shady his life. As Zoe got the door open, Lil Shawn rammed the car causing the couple to jerk forward and Zoe to fall from the car. Seeing this Shady leapt from the car blazing.

"Blah, blah, blah, blah!" Shady let out four rounds at Lil Shawn and Mylo. Each round missing it's target. Shady was rusty. Very rusty! He had the element of surprise in his advantage, but this form of [art of] war didn't help the older Crip because this was a wasted opportunity and four fewer slugs he had to protect he and Zoe.

Lil Shawn and Mylo both dove from the Honda with their pistols drawn. Zoe had fallen to the ground and in a state of shock laid there as Shady shot. He ran around the car and grabbed Zoe and took cover in front of the car. Lil Shawn and Mylo were both now on their feet ducking behind the hood of the Honda. They did not know what just happened or what went wrong, but they knew one thing, Shady had to die tonight.

Shady looked at Zoe ducking low behind the hood of his car. She was shaking like dice in Vegas trying to dial 9-1-1 with her cellphone. Shady snapped. "Zoe, what the fuck are you doing?! This shit ain't like in the movies! This shit is real life! Start thinking with your survival skills. These are some young niggas, you going to be dead before the police get here. Now, when I say run, run and don't stop!"

Tears had filled Zoe's eyes and were running down her cheeks in rivers. This stuff she'd seen only in scary movies. She'd heard about a few criminal cases as such from her criminal lawyer friends, but she was a civil attorney, all the violence she was not immune to. She could not come to terms how she had got herself into such a situation.

"Run! Zoe, run!" Shady popped over the hood and saw Lil Shawn and Mylo were laying low behind their car trunk. Zoe best time at survival was now. "Run!"

Zoe took off towards her neighbor's yard like the initial plan. Shady leapt from behind the hood and covered. Upon seeing movement, the Tiny Mites started blazing. "Pop, pop, pop, pop!"

"Boom, boom, boom, boom!"

"Blah, blah, blah, blah!"

The shootout began. The two Tiny Mites versus Shady. Bullets flew every which way. None hitting it's target until Mylo aimed his gun at Zoe Miller as she ran and sent two slugs her way. The first shot

148

flew inches above her head. The second one grazed a piece of her ear. She yelled "Aargh!" in agony and fear. She lost her footing and fell to the ground. As she hit the ground Shady's eyes widened. He and Lil Shawn had been ducking back and forth behind the cars playing laser tag, but neither one of these Crips could shoot. Their accuracy was zero for ten. Bullets were filling the cars and nearby houses.

Seeing his first love and mother to his unborn child go down. Shady ran from his cover and took aim at Mylo. "Blah, blah, blah!" He shot three times hitting Mylo in the shoulder blade. The impact from the slug was in and out, but the younger Crip lost his grip of his gun and this gave Shady enough time to make it over to Zoe. He lifted her back to her feet again yelled "Run!" as he covered her.

Lil Shawn still using his car as cover, placed both hands on the handle of his .9mm and in the standard police stance over the trunk of the car, he sent in an entourage of bullets at Shady. This time each bullet met its mark.

"Pop, pop, pop, pop, pop, pop, pop!"

"Blah, blah, blah, blah!"

"Click. Click. Click."

The two Crips shot it out until their clips were empty. As Shady sent his last four slugs at Lil Shawn he took bullet after bullet. His upper torso seemed like a bullet magnet after the first impact landed at the middle of his chest. Seven bullets ripped in and out of Shady sending him spilling to his knees. Shady shot back at Lil Shawn but the Honda protected the young soldier.

After Shady had hit the ground and his gun fell out of his hand he tried to crawl to safety. He was still breathing. Shady was a fighter. He had to stay alive to see Zoe give birth to his offspring. He had to muster the strength to get up and run. He couldn't die, not today. He was too young. He had to live. He had just begun to live right. He was doing everything legit. *Get up and run*, he told himself. *I can't go out like this.* He tried to get up but his body was dead weight. *Damn, come on Shady.* he thought *You can't go out like this.*

"Just come on home son, everything going to be alright."

As he fought to stay alive his mother's voice roared in his head. His breathing became slow and hard. It felt like someone was suffocating him from within. The dark cloud of death moved over Shady as Lil Shawn drew the two revolvers he had holstered at waist level and jogged over to Shady to finish the kill.

"Yeah!" Lil Shawn said hovering over Shady. "What you thought that we weren't going to find out that the Tiny Loc Bastardz was plotting against us? This Tiny Mites or Nothing!"

"BOOM!"

"BOOM!"

"BOOM!"

The two .357 Revolvers barked loud and proud throughout the night air sending Shady to rejoin his mother in the afterlife. Zoe Miller heard the final three gunshots as she made it into the door of her house. As the shots rang out, her heart skipped a beat and her body became weak. Death had claimed stake on half of her heart. And Shady's flesh and blood started twirling in her stomach. She vomited on her way to the phone. She dialed 9-1-1.

Lil Shawn got his man and went to check on Mylo who was leaned over next to the Honda gripping his pistol in the right hand and holding his right shoulder with the left. "You alright?" he asked.

"Yeah, that bitch ass nigga shot me cuz." Mylo said in agony. "But let's get the fuck out outta here. We got our man."

"You damn right we did. Tiny Mites or Nothing. Now let's go get you stitched up and celebrate."

Chapter 23

"Okay, yall hide in the bathroom," Kioshi told P and Sheik after Pooh hung up the phone with Mylo. "Them niggaz should be pulling up any minute. Pooh added "They so young and dumb, they bragging about just having a shootout with one of their homies and Mylo got shot, but it ain't bad. It went in and out..."

As P sat listening to Kioshi and Pooh explain what they just heard from the two Tiny Mites, he could not help but think about Shady. "If them two niggaz had a shootout with anyone from their hood it have to be Shady or Big Wrap," he told himself. "Let me call Shady and check on him."

P retrieve his cell phone from his pocket and placed the Desert Eagle pistol he had grip tight on his lap. He scrolled through his contacts than dialed Shady's number upon finding it. Shady's phone rung and rung. He got the voice mail. "Damn," he hissed. He called back.

Riiiiinnnnng!

Riiiiiinnnnng!

Riiiiiinnnnng!

"God sent me an Angel from the heaven's above..." Amanda Perez's hot single 'Angel' played in the background of Shady's voice mail as he said: "I'm not available right now, please leave me a message and I'll surely get back to you as soon as possible."

Due to the situation, this was a sad song. Even though Shady played the song as his greeting on his voicemail playing homage to his mother and Zoe Miller; this would eventually be the song that brings many terse to the eyes of his loved ones. Because in the hood, word spread fast like a wildfire. Within an hour of Shady's death, the whole community was at the crime scene. It started from P's calls going unanswered. He then called Laurell who was over the bowl vomiting. She figured it was symptoms from a hard pregnancy until she received the call from P. After hanging up P , Laurell called Big Wrap. Big Wrap called Shady's call phone. The voice mail picked up. Then, he called the unknown number Shady called him from a few weeks back when they met at Friday's. Zoe Miller answered on the third ring petrified and sobbing. She confirmed that Shady was dead. Big Wrap tad her don't talk over the phone. She gave him the directions to her house and before the coroners could arrive to take Shady's body to the morgue, the whole hood was at the scene standing behind the yellow crime scene tape. Even Momma Mary and Maria was in attendance. Once again, the streets had claimed the life of a young black man. Another mother's baby. Momma Mary said a silent prayer "Lord, please be with Andre. But please don't let my son die before me."

Five minutes after P called Laurell she called him back with the news. "Dead!" He repeated through the phone.

"Yes," Laurell sobbed. "They killed my brother. He's dead!"

P just shook his head he Couldn't believe Shady was dead. It seemed like it was just yesterday they were at Roscoe's Chicken and Waffle. *Damn, that nigga didn't deserve to die*, he thought. *He was on some positive shit. But damn that's why I ain't tryna go clean because it seems like as soon as a nigga do, he end up dead or getting killed.*

"He's dead!" Laurell sobbed. "My brother is dead! P, my brother is dead!"

Laurell was lost in a world of sorrow. She repeated herself ten times before P told her he would get back at her. He hung the phone, looked at his crew and his eyes read: MURDER, MURDER, KILL, KILL!

Chapter 24

The dumpster is in the alley.

Check.

The smokers who moved it from the hotel to the alley is gone.

Check.

The scene is clear.

Check.

Now, all I got to do is wait on these two suckas to pull up.

Keisha sat in the driver seat of the getaway car outside of the hotel where she, Kioshi, and Pooh had committed various malice acts, but this time once again her younger brother had her and her crew a mission to kill. Conspiring to end someone's life wasn't fun nor cool, but when it came to getting paid, to Keisha it was by any means necessary. And in addition to that anyone crossed her brother crossed her. Keisha sat patiently waiting for the home-going arrival of Lil Shawn and Mylo. And even though, the pair of Tiny Mites were the best friends of Brandon, she planned to play a part in their death. To her, blood was thicker than water and cum.

Nothing come before my family, she told herself. *Yea people say blood is thicker than water and cum is thicker than blood, but not me. My Lil brother before any nigga or bitch I ever fuck with.*

Just as Keisha told herself that, Lil Shawn and Mylo pulled into the hotel parking lot in a white Honda Accord. The car had multiple bullet holes in it. She shook her head. *These stupid muthafuckaz driving around in the same car they just killed somebody out of. Luckily, this is a bullshit hotel that everyone in the city knows the cameras don't work or these two stupid-ass niggaz would be on camera getting out of the car the crime was committed out of. I swear I hate clown-ass niggaz.*

Keisha grabbed her phone as Lil Shawn parked a few parking stalls over from her. She had occupied the last stall to be at the back exit of the hotel next to the alley to make sure everything went as planned. She called Kioshi.

"They just pulled up," she said into the phone after Kioshi picked up.

"Yeah, we see 'em from the room. Me and Pooh on our way down."

Kioshi hung up the phone and looked at P. "We bout to go get 'em right now. When I say let's play a game y'all come out."

"Just make sure y'all get them niggaz in here," P responded.

"Because if we don't know how to do nothing else, we know how to hit niggaz over the head," Sheik added with his signature Devilish grin. Sheik was a complete fool and wild nigga. This was the type of situations he lived for.

Kioshi and Pooh exited the room and walked to the elevator. They rode the elevator from the tenth floor to the lobby. As always the sleepy front desk clerk barely even looked up from the book he was reading. This day he was reading a book titled 'Murder She Wrote'. Behind the book disguise, Kioshi realized the clerk was sleep. She smiled inwardly. *This makes our plan easier, but I wonder do he always be sleep when I see him reading? Or is that book just boring?*

Outside of the hotel, the midnight air was chilly which brought chills throughout both girls bodies. "Whoo, it's cold as fuck out here," Pooh said to no one in particular. "Y'all need to hurry up," she said to Lil Shawn and Mylo as they approached.

"Bitch, you best slow yo' roll," Lil Shawn uttered. "Don't you see my nigga injured. Which is more important, you being cold or my nigga being shot?"

Ugh! I hate young-dumb-stupid-ass niggaz, Kioshi thought. She glanced at Pooh and they both were thinking the same thing. *Yea we going to show who's the bitch in a minute.*

"Baby, don't worry about her, you here for me; so let's get to know each other better and it looks like you could go for a good massage first."

Lil Shawn looked at Kioshi and bit down on his bottom lip. He just could not wait to fuck the shit out of her. *I'm bout to fuck the shit out of this thick ass red bone and have her begging for more.*

Mylo walked hunched over holding his shoulder. "I need some Aspirin or something," he said to Pooh. "Y'all got some pain pills up there? If not, we gon need to go to the liquor store cause a nigga need some drink too."

"We got everything in the room," Pooh lied. "We even got a first aid kit up there."

The quartet entered the hotel, walked by the sleepy front desk clerk, and to the elevator. They rode to the tenth floor. This was the last floor of the ten story high-rise hotel. At room 2187, Kioshi inserted the key. She entered the room followed by Lil Shawn gripping her waist and humping her butt as they walked. He just knew he was about to send Kioshi to la-la land and beyond.

As the pair of couples settled into the room; each occupying a bed in the double bed suite. This was deja vu to Pooh. This reminded her of BO and

Smooth, and how she and Keisha had rocked them to sleep. She looked at Mylo and said "Take off your shirt. Let me see how bad your wound is." Truth to the matter, Pooh wanted to make sure Mylo wasn't armed. And after she helped him out of his shirt, she realized that he wasn't. She assumed he left it in the car. She secretly gave a thumbs up to Kioshi on the other side of the room.

Kioshi got right to work on Lil Shawn. Little did he know all the grinding and dry humping he was doing on her big booty was her way of determining that he was armed. Every time she would grind her round ass back against his thrust, she felt with her hands and rear where his pistols were located. *Damn, this young crazy muhfucka got two guns,* she thought. *But I got a trick up my sleeve for his ass. I mean, what nigga gon' tell me no.*

"Wait! Wait!!" She stopped on a dime and turned to him. "If we going to go any farther with this you gotta put them guns up because they fucking up the mood."

Lil Shawn was green, even a blind person could have seen he was a puppy trying to be a big dog. He was a rookie to the streets, and this rookie mistake of thinking with his small head instead of his big head would be a deadly mistake. Just as Kioshi wanted, Lil Shawn replied, "Damn, cuzz, let me put these in the drawer right quick."

Lil Shawn disarmed himself and flopped on the bed. Kioshi hopped on top of him. She straddled her latest victim of seduction and smiled inwardly. *Another one bites the dust*. She looked at Pooh who was on the other side examining Mylo's flesh wound. They nodded at each other and Kioshi said,"Let's play a game."

Lil Shawn forever the horn-dog replied, "What kinda game?" He was thinking all the freaky things he and Mylo could do to the two sexy redbones. But as quick as the thought arose it was gone. P and Sheik emerged out of the bathroom with their pistols pointed.

"My game," P informed using the "Art Of War's", 'Element Of Surprise', on the two young goons. P headed straight over to Lil Shawn and grabbed him by the neck like the wrestler da Undertaker. He pointed his .45 at Lil Shawn's temple and stared him in the eyes. "Nigga, you barked up the wrong tree!"

Crack!

P pistol whipped him over the head. Kioshi went to the nightstand and grabbed the two revolvers out the drawer. She kept one and handed Pooh one. Sheik had Mylo face down on the floor with his foot on his neck. The two Tiny Mites went from behind the gun to the barrel of the gun.

Crack!

160

P pistol whipped Lil Shawn repeatedly over the
head until blood started to gush out. The young
teeny bopper let out groans of pain. Things weren't
moving fast now, everything was becoming slow
motion like a movie. P shoved the terrified so-called
head nigga of the notorious Tiny Mites into a chair.
He ordered Kioshi to handcuff him. P sensed the toy
gangster was plastic as soon as he walked out of the
bathroom. To him, Lil Shawn just laid down as
soon as he seen them. The self-proclaimed hardcore
young gangsta didn't even put up a fight. P wanted
to just split his wig and keep it moving , but he
remembered what Dee Bastard had taught him
when they killed Bo and Smooth. It's easy to kill a
man, but understanding the enemy and learning him
before committing the murder is the hardest. One
would say 'if it's worth fighting for, it's worth dying
for, and if it's worth dying for there's nothing to talk
about; but not this go around. P needed answers. If
not for himself, at least, for Dee Bastard. He knew
his mentor was going to need some type of closure
losing both of his childhood friends.

After Lil Shawn was handcuffed and Mylo
released from the boot to his neck, the two Tiny
Mites sat shaking like dice in Vegas. "Alright,
before we take this any further let's get straight to
business. What made y'all two niggas and Brandon,
do what y'all did? The Tiny Mites and Tiny Locs
suppose to be family. Why you niggas take it this
far?"

Lil Shawn's eyes widened and Mylo swallowed spit. This was, once again deja vu. Everyone knew BO and Smooth suffered the same fate when they were under the gun after committing the same offense: Death Before Betrayal act. To P, their reaction was part of the understanding that their time of existence was limited. Lil Shawn spoke, "That's the something we thought." His words came out in a low utter.

P shook his head with his arms folded across his chest gripping his gun. His trigger finger was burning like it was on fire. Sheik stood behind him with the same burning sensation, but he also learned from Dee Bastard the please of killing a man didn't come just from pulling the trigger; it was from bringing the bitch out of the so-called gangster.

"Okay, let me understand something," P said. "If you thought y'all was family why would y'all kill y'all folks then?"

Lil Shawn could not think past go. His gangsterism wasn't built like that. Beads of sweat popped through the pores of his forehead. He decided to explain the situation as he knew it. "Man, BT told me that the Tiny Loc's were tripping on us. Something like how Bo and Smooth tripped on them..."

After Lil Shawn explained the situation and beef, P shook his head. In a way, he felt bad for the two flunkies. He remembered something Bo told Dee Bastard before the dark cloud of death moved over him. The dead man words roared through his head. "From an OG to a YG, history repeats itself. This shit is ALL OVER POWER."

"Look, I'ma make this easy on us all. BT is a snitch. He played you and your crew. He told on BC and Dee Bastard. The nigga is walking on thin ice, so he used y'all to get the heat off of him.."

P paused letting his words sink in. He saw that Lil Shawn and Mylo both knew they were dead as doorknobs. The two Tiny Mites didn't know P or Sheik from Adam but they did recall seeing the duo at the funeral. They assumed P and Sheik had to be undercover TLB's. There had been many rumors that the TLBs were connected and had members all over. *Damn, the TLBs ain't just a 4 Trey clique,* Mylo thought. He was still shaking nonstop. He'd never been in a situation as such. Being the one under the gun was totally different from being the one behind the trigger. He stayed quiet.

"But this what we going to do," P continued. "BT is upstairs on the roof. We got him tied to a chair up there, so I'ma give y'all a chance to go ask him why he play y'all."

P lied. He needed to get Lil Shawn and Mylo up to the roof without incident. The two Tiny Mites agreed. they figured confronting BT would be there

163

only chance at survival. The quartet ushered the two toy gangsters out of the room and to the elevator. Lil Shawn and Mylo were still handcuffed behind their back. The hotel was empty and quiet. The quartet had their pistols tucked at waist level and walked as if nothing out of the ordinary was going on.

They rode the elevator to the roof and pushed the walking dead towards their final destination: the ledge. Lil Shawn surveyed the perimeter and realized BT was nowhere in sight. He sensed death lurking like a thief in the night. Within less than an hour Karma had come back and haunted him and his boy. Just as Shady's body wad rattled with bullets so was theirs.

After the quartet shoved the walking dead men towards the ledge, they formed a gun line in front of them. "Turn around," P ordered.

"Aint no use of looking at the ten story fall you niggas about to take, if y'all try to jump," Sheik said.

The two Tiny Mites faced their would be killers for the last time. The firing squad on P's command aim and fired.

Boom, blah, boom, blah, pop, pop, pop!

A barrage of bullets shot out of each gun turning Lil Shawn's and Mylo's lifeless bodies into swiss cheese; the force of the bullets pushing their corpses from the ledge of the roof ten stories down into the dumpster.

"Touchdown!" Keisha said, after the bodies landed into the dumpster and the lids closed. She started the engine and pulled to the entrance of the hotel. She and the quartet vanished unseen. P told himself, *You live by the gun, you die by the gun. I can do this shit 100 days, 100 nights.*

Chapter 25

"Damn!" "Damn!!" Detective Gilmore burst as he watched the morning news. "Damn!!!"

"In Los Angeles, a series of murders has plagued the city, in which two gangs has pledged to each kill each other for 100 days and 100 nights says LAPD. Los Angeles District Attorney office is demanding answers from LAPD..."

Detective Gilmore grabbed his phone and dialed BT.

Riiiiinnnnng!

Riiiiinnnnng!

"Hello!"

"What's the hell is going on out there?" Detective Gilmore asked. His plan had backed fired. His fifteen minutes of fame was now up for grabs. He had to get his hands on a suspect fast.

BT looked at his cell phone and hung up. He was on Interstate 5 headed far away from Los Angels as possible. He tossed the cell phone out of the window and kept pushing. H knew it was only a matter of time before the same people who killed Lil Shawn and Mylo come for him. Life in Los Angeles was a living hell. Death was only around the corner.And with Dee Bastard due to be released soon no telling what was bound to happen.

Click!

Upon seeing he'd been hung up on, Detective Gilmore couldn't do anything but shake his head in defeat. He smiled to himself , *Can't win 'em all, but I still got some tricks up my sleeves. I'll get 'em all sooner than later. You live by the gun, you rot in a cell.*

The corrupted cop sat in his living room plotting his next move. He was like the evil genius when it came to destroying the lives of young black men in the city of Lost Angels. He knew with him at the helm the saga would continue...

Chapter 26

Dee Bastard sat in his cell thinking about his two best friends, once again, he was caught at a crossroad in his life. He's always been taught an eye for an eye and if someone hit you, you hit them back ten times harder. *Bastard Child was an asshole and wildcat at times but he didn't deserve to die. Neither did Shady. We were on some get money positive shit,* he told himself. *But like R. Kelly say in his song. 'Dear homies we done been through a whole lot of shit together. From running these streets to being down for whatever…'*

Dee Bastard sat up on his bunk writing about his childhood friends. This was the only way he could vent. The pain he felt from losing not one but two friends was unexplainable. His whole crew was gone. He was literally the last of a dying breed.

"Damn, BC, just tell me what went wrong up there in that cell," he spoke out loud to himself. It was a quarter to five in the morning and he'd been up all night writing, crying, and reminiscing. Tears ran down his cheeks in rivers. He was glad OG Ronnie Mack was sleep. He couldn't see himself crying in front of another man. But his emotions were running high and he could care less who seen him cry at that point in his life.

"Damn, Shady, just tell me what happened that fast?"

He sobbed. "How could I just lose both of my niggaz like this? Damn, God! What am I to do now? I try to do right but seems like only bad is my reward when I do good. I'm trying to be TLW, The Leader of the West, but it seem like Dee Bastard, the notorious Crip gang leader, is my only hope. I want to get out and live a righteous life, but I can't live right without righting them wrongs."

Dee Bastard shook his head. He couldn't believe his life had taken another drastic change. He remembered vowing to change if God ever gave him a chance at freedom, but here it was he had a release date months away soon approaching and he was once again stuck at a cross road. He didn't know what was going on. Or what God had in store for him. But like Proverbs 16:9 says "A man's heart plan his way, but the Lord directs his steps." The questions of doubt and hopelessness started to kick in.

Damn, what the fuck happened' he thought. 'What's going to happen when I get out? Am I'm going to stay focused or is trouble going to come knocking? But then again what about BC and

Shady? Do I let their murders go unanswered or do I ride for my niggaz? What about Laurell and my unborn? What about Zoe Miller and Shady's unborn? What about my mama? What about Brandon? What about BT? What about that detective? It's like damn if I do, damn if I don't!

Dee Bastard sat up in that cell thinking over every possibility that could go wrong. After he ended the chapter to his book, he said a quick prayer "Lord, I know I am not right, but I am far from wrong. Please guide my life in the best way you see fit and keep me strong. I don't know what tomorrow brings, but I am full of hopes and dreams. Still pushing for TLW, but the Devil love for Dee Bastard to fail you. As I close my eyes to sleep I ask that you keep me humble and you keep me safe. Amen"

Dee Bastard closed his eyes to rest his neck, but sleep didn't come easy. He knew deep within life on the streets wasn't going to be peaceful. he knew revenge was a must. He knew his conscious wasn't going to let him live right. He had to retaliate the deaths of his two childhood friends. The beast within him needed his just due. The dark side of Dee Bastard knew that it was loyalty over love and respect before hugs.

"I gotta do something," he told himself. "But this time Imma do it right and make all my folks happy. How I'm going to do it? I don't know, yet,

but as of right now I just gotta wait til I get to that bridge."

Dee Bastard fell asleep with sweet dreams of still being The Leader of the West, but would his alter ego eventually be the downfall of the legendary TLB founder?

The Saga Continue…

To Live & Die In LA 3

Coming Soon

Early 2017

TO LIVE & DIE IN LA 2   TERRY L. WROTEN